Delightfully Different

D. S. WALKER

iUniverse, Inc.
Bloomington

Delightfully Different

This is a work of fiction. All of the characters, names, incidents, organizations, and dialogue in this novel are either the products of the author's imagination or are used fictitiously.

iUniverse books may be ordered through booksellers or by contacting:

iUniverse
1663 Liberty Drive
Bloomington, IN 47403
www.iuniverse.com
1-800-Authors (1-800-288-4677)

Because of the dynamic nature of the Internet, any Web addresses or links contained in this book may have changed since publication and may no longer be valid. The views expressed in this work are solely those of the author and do not necessarily reflect the views of the publisher, and the publisher hereby disclaims any responsibility for them.

ISBN: 978-1-4502-6050-3 (pbk)
ISBN: 978-1-4502-6051-0 (cloth)
ISBN: 978-1-4502-6052-7 (ebk)

Library of Congress Control Number: 2010913920

Printed in the United States of America

iUniverse rev. date: 8/18/2011

Grateful acknowledgment is made to the authors of the material listed below for granting permission to use excerpts of the following previously published material:

Fox, Mem. 1993. *Time for Bed*. San Diego, New York, London: Gulliver Books. Harcourt Brace & Company.

Kirby, Barbara L. http://www.aspergersyndrome.org/Articles/The-OASIS-Asperger-Syndrome-Guide-for-Teachers---L.aspx.

Romanowski Bashe, Patricia, and Barbara L. Kirby. 2005. *The OASIS Guide to Asperger Syndrome*. New York: Crown Publishers.

Stillman, William. 2006. *Autism and the God Connection: Redefining the Autistic Experience through Extraordinary Accounts of Spiritual Giftedness*. Naperville, Illinois: Sourcebooks, Inc.

To all of the delightfully different children of the world. God bless each of you!

Acknowledgments

Thanks to God and all of his angels on earth and in heaven. You led me to the right people and places to get help with making this book a reality.

Special thanks to Margery Jacobson, who was there from the start. You are truly an angel. You encouraged me and showed faith in me throughout this process. You offered sound advice when asked. I am truly so grateful to you for all of your help and support.

Thanks to my wonderful husband and children. I could not have done this without your love and support.

Thanks to my sister-in-law, K.T., for her support and suggestions.

Thanks to all of my close friends and extended family—you know who you are—who supported this endeavor and who kept me going by asking me, "How is the book coming?"

Special thanks to G.D. and B.D. You helped in so many ways, including reading a draft copy of this story. You're truly the best!

Thanks to R.M. for agreeing to be my final proofreader. From the day we met, you have been there for my entire family.

Thanks to John M. and Bob W. for their advice on how to get the book in print.

Thanks to Barb Kirby and Patty Romanowski Bashe for their kind responses to my requests and for allowing me to include quotes from their book and also for helping so many. Special thanks to Barb for creating the OASIS Web site mentioned in my introduction and to Patty for continuing her research.

Thanks to William Stillman for granting me permission to quote from one of his wonderful books. Thanks also for writing two more books on the same subject, which I still need to read.

Thanks to Janet Treasure for her kind response to my request and for allowing me to use information from her study and for doing the study in the first place.

Thanks to all of the authors listed as resources in the back of this book. This book would not have been possible without you.

Thanks to all who care for and love these delightfully different souls.

Special thanks to Mem Fox, who graciously granted permission for me to quote up to four pages of her wonderful children's book *Time for Bed* in my story.

Thanks to my editorial consultant, George Nedeff, for addressing my concerns and helping me to achieve my goals.

Thanks to my editor, Lynn Everett, for her wonderful insights and advice. You helped me achieve my goals.

Introduction

Asperger's Syndrome (AS) is a neurological disorder on the autism spectrum. The CDC currently estimates that an average of one in 110 children in the United States have an autism spectrum disorder. While Hans Asperger first recognized the symptoms in the 1940s, the term Asperger's syndrome was not used until 1981. The diagnosis was not even recognized in the United States until 1994.

Because it is still a relatively new diagnosis, it continues to be either missed or misdiagnosed by pediatricians. Psychologists, psychiatrists, and neurologists may even misdiagnose these children. The parent has to continue digging when the diagnosis does not seem to fit the child.

It is important to note that before 1994, it was believed to be an obscure diagnosis. Physicians were not taught what symptoms to look for prior to this. Unlike with autism, there is no clinically significant delay in language. Frequently, the diagnosis is not obtained until children start school, and girls may not be diagnosed until puberty.

The following is a portion of a letter from *The Oasis Guide to Asperger Syndrome* by Patricia Romanowski Bashe and Barbara L. Kirby. They recommend parents of children with Asperger's use it as a guide when writing to their child's teacher.

> Every child with AS is unique. No two have the same pattern of behaviors, skills, or deficits. A technique or approach that worked for one child may not necessarily work for the next, or what worked last month may not work today. (403–408)

The entire letter can be found on the following Web site: http://www.aspergersyndrome.org/Articles/The-OASIS-Asperger-Syndrome-Guide-for-Teachers---L.aspx.[1]

Parents and teachers often have to play detective to determine the cause

---

1 Copyright PRBookworks and Barbara L. Kirby.

of the sometimes puzzling behaviors of children with Asperger's syndrome. They may seem to get angry for no reason. When the parents conduct their own investigation, they learn there is a reason. Sometimes it can be something simple. For example, the child is already overloaded from keeping it together in school all day, so when she gets in the car and the radio is too loud for her sensitive hearing, she may react angrily.

Symptoms can include literal and rigid thinking; direct language that seems rude; perfectionism; sensory issues; poor motor skills, including balance and coordination; problems with making eye contact or prolonged staring; social phobias along with deficiencies in social skills; and the need for routine, which leads to difficulty with change. Many of these children have sensory sensitivity to touch, smell, bright lights, sounds, and even taste. If parents don't understand, they may think their children are being disrespectful or worse. If they see a psychologist for anger issues, the sensory issues may be overlooked and the children may be misdiagnosed.

Girls might be misdiagnosed with depression or attention deficit disorder. Boys might be given the diagnosis of bipolar disorder or attention deficit hyperactive disorder. Children of both sexes can be misdiagnosed as oppositional defiant if they exhibit symptoms of anger.

In girls, symptoms frequently are not noticed until puberty. One theory is that their symptoms are subtler or that their symptoms appear less severe. Girls may be better at verbalizing their emotions and thus are less likely to be physically aggressive in response to negative emotions, such as confusion, frustration, or anger. Children who are more aggressive are more likely to be referred for a diagnostic assessment.

Many believe the reason girls are not diagnosed sooner is that they are also more likely to copy their peers and to appear to be shy. It is only when girls go through puberty that their symptoms become more obvious. Sensory issues might cause them to dress differently than their peers. Before puberty, clothing might not be a noticeable difference.

These issues become more obvious in middle school, when most teenage girls want to wear more feminine clothes while girls with Asperger's steer toward more comfortable clothing, like athletic shorts and loose-fitting T-shirts. Sensitivity to touch likely will prevent them from wearing popular styles of clothing. Loud, popular music may hurt their ears if they have sensitive hearing. Perfumes may burn their noses, and fluorescent lights might hurt their eyes so that shopping is not fun. They might not like the smell of chlorine from the pool or the feel of sand at the beach. Sunshine might severely hurt their eyes.

Their social awkwardness can also become more obvious when the parents are no longer the ones doing the planning. Talking on the phone is hard for them. The volume might be too loud, or holding something against their ears might cause too much pressure if their ears are sensitive to touch.

A recent study conducted by Janet Treasure, professor of psychiatry at the Institute of Psychiatry, King's College, London, showed that approximately a fifth of girls diagnosed with anorexia have autistic spectrum features. She noted they exhibited rigidity and perfectionism in childhood. She indicated that anorexia may be a form of female Asperger's.

The above study presents a real concern, since even girls on the spectrum without anorexia can have issues with their diets because of limited food choices due to their sensitivity issues. They might not like the smell, texture, or taste of certain foods.

Of note, Asperger's syndrome can also have many positive aspects. Kids with Asperger's are honest and reliable. They do not follow the crowd when they know something is wrong. They have integrity. Most are intelligent and talented. The ability to focus on a subject of interest allows them to accomplish things far beyond the average person. Excellent rote memory is also common from a very young age, and some even have photographic memories. Early on, they may have vocabulary well beyond their years, which is why Asperger's syndrome is sometimes called "the little professor syndrome." Perfect pitch, which allows some to be gifted musically, is another trait of Asperger's.

I firmly believe people on the autistic spectrum are sensitive, spiritual souls, who are here to teach us lessons about being better human beings.

Several books, including *Autism and the God Connection* by William Stillman, have been written about autistic kids having spiritual gifts. They seem to know things well beyond what their age and "limitations" would allow. Some parents believe that their children chose them. Mia, the main character in my story, would be on the autistic spectrum. I chose to have her start out as a spirit watching her mother from heaven because of the spiritual connection.

While all of the characters in this book exist only in the author's imagination, bullying is a very real issue in our schools today. Many of the victims have some form of learning disability and/or a neurological disorder, such as Mia's sensory sensitivity with features of Asperger's syndrome. AS kids are often victims of bullying because of their differences. Sometimes, they do not realize that they are victims until things escalate.

Patricia Romanowski Bashe, MS Ed., and Barbara L. Kirby devoted a section to bullying and teasing in their book *The OASIS Guide to Asperger Syndrome*.[2] They write, "Persons with AS and related disorders are even more likely to be targets of teasing, harassment, and bullying of both a verbal and physical nature" (371).

2 See pages 371–374.

They tell of a mother whose son was called a "retard" and then pushed on the playground. The teacher did not believe the victim and then added, "Well, your son is different, and it bothers the other children" (372).

The authors acknowledge, "Other parents have reported numerous occasions in which the responses to their complaints about teasing have amounted to blaming the child with AS for 'bringing it on himself' by essentially being who he is" (372).

Finally, they explain,

> It is imperative that our children and their siblings be protected from both physical and emotional abuse from anyone. One hundred percent of the adults with Asperger Syndrome who have participated in the OASIS message boards or contacted Barb through the Web site report the devastating effects these kinds of incidents had on their lives (372–373).

Many teachers and school counselors misunderstand these children. Some even cause more harm in trying to help when they do not understand. That is why I created the character Mr. Nikula. He is not a bad person. He really does not understand. My hope is that this book will inspire people to become more tolerant as they become more informed.

I utilized several sources to help me create the character of Mia, including the books mentioned above and several other books about Asperger's syndrome and sensory sensitivity. They are listed at the back of the book. They are all excellent resources for parents and children who may be experiencing life as a delightfully different spirit.

Officer John is also a fictional character. However, there is a real group of police officers who work with a group called Bully Police. Their Web site is BullyPolice.org.

Remember, every life has a purpose. We are all unique in some way, even if we do not admit it. Be grateful for who you are and for who your children are. Help them to learn to cope in this world. Use whatever resources are necessary to help them. However, do not try to make them like the rest of the world. Help them to be proud of who they are.

Part I

Chapter I
FAMILY DIFFERENCES

Mia

My name is Mia Lung. This is the story of the first eighteen years of my life. It is also the story of my mother and of my family's love.

From the time I started school, I have lived my life knowing I was different from my peers, and I often wondered why. I blamed it on my mother, because I am the product of a mixed-culture marriage. I believed the reason I was different was because my mother was Caucasian. Most of my friends were 100 percent Asian.

On my mother's side, I can trace my family back to before the Revolutionary War, which is mostly a good thing. However, my mother's family settled in the Deep South after the Revolutionary War. As my mother explains, they were therefore on the "wrong side" during the Civil War. Some of her ancestors owned slaves, so Mom is both proud and embarrassed by her heritage. This may explain why she usually tells people she is from Montana, which is where she lived when she met my dad.

My dad's family is Chinese. Ah Gung's (Chinese for "grandfather") family has lived in Hawaii for over four generations. My dad is either the fourth or the fifth generation, depending on whether you use Ah Gung's father's or mother's side. On Ah Ma's (Chinese for "grandmother") side, I am only the third generation born on American soil. Therefore, Ah Ma expected all of her grandchildren to strive not just to do their best, but also to be the best at everything they did to make our ancestors proud because they had sacrificed so much to come to America.

If you have ever read the book or seen the movie *The Joy Luck Club*, then you have an idea of what it was like to be Ah Ma's granddaughter. If you have not, then suffice it to say, Ah Ma made me feel like I had to be the best at everything, yet she never told me why she did this. Because of the way she talked to us, there was competition among all of her grandchildren. For instance, if I told her that I was taking piano lessons, she told me that my cousin had just received a medal for swimming. If I got an A on my report card, she told me how many A's my cousin had gotten. It didn't matter that I was older and the subjects were harder. She did this for everything.

Chinese culture is rather complicated. Honor and respect for family and family ancestors is important. Equally important is saving face. Face is how we appear to others. Outward appearances can sometimes seem more important than true character.

I don't believe it was Ah Ma's intention to make me feel less valued or less loved than my cousins. Still, this was how I felt when she always changed the subject to my cousins' accomplishments.

Because of cultural differences, my parents' marriage did not always receive full support from their families. Both families had concerns, and neither side understood that some of their values were the same.

Mom's parents told her that they would not be around if this marriage failed because they were older. Grandma also cried because Mom would be living so far away.

Grandpa even reminded Mom that it was once illegal for white people to marry Asians. Mom took offense to this, and Grandpa had to explain that he did not mean it that way. He just wanted Mom to understand that things might be hard because of this.

Mom told him that she and Dad had decided to live in Hawaii for just that reason. She assured him that lots of people in Hawaii had multicultural marriages.

Dad's family asked Mom questions about her Southern family like, "Did they own slaves?" Mom took offense to this since obviously *she* had never owned slaves. She grew up respecting all people. The implication that her family was racist just because they lived in the South was upsetting to her. Dad also told Mom that his mom always wanted him to marry a Chinese girl.

This alone would be hard enough for some couples to overcome, but to add to my parents' stress, God gave them me. Mom said I was a gift from God sent to teach her patience. My mom always loved me, even during times when I was difficult to understand. Because Dad's family didn't openly show affection except to babies, it was harder for him to show affection as I grew up. This caused me to doubt his love for me.

Okay, I have given you a basic overview of my family heritage. Now I must start at the very beginning of my story, so you can really understand who I am.

Chapter II
Choosing Mom

Mia

You see, I was with Mom before I was born. I watched her from heaven for years, waiting for her to have a child so I could be born.

I first learned about Mom when she was only twelve years old. She had many losses in her life that year, including her Grandma Laura. When Great-Grandma Laura died, she and I became friends. She told me how Francesca was such a sweet girl that she hated to leave her. She said she knew that Francesca was special the day she met her as a newborn baby. The two of them had a special bond. Great-Grandma Laura learned I would get to choose my mother. She begged me to observe Francesca for a time to decide if she should be my mother.

So unbeknownst to my future mother, I studied her from heaven. Great-Grandma was right; she was special. She had flyaway, silky, copper-colored hair and beautiful green eyes that lit up when she smiled. I observed how much she loved all of her family and her pets.

I remember one day in particular. It was a cloudy, cold day in early March. Francesca couldn't have been more than fourteen because I remember her little sister Angie was nine. They were sitting close together on the brown couch in their living room. The pretty, blue ruffled curtains that matched the color of Angie's eyes were closed. The only light in the room was from the TV. A scary show about vampires was on, and Angie screamed and buried her head in Francesca's shoulder. Francesca stroked Angie's honey-colored hair and told her it would be okay. Then, even though the show wasn't over, she got up from the couch to turn off the TV and turn on the lights. She pulled back the curtain and said, "Angie, you know it's just a show. It's not even dark yet.

I see Mom and Paul coming up the driveway. You know our linebacker-built brother won't let anything happen to you. You are safe."

Francesca could have made fun of Angie's fear or refused to turn the TV off until the end of the show. Instead, she showed concern for Angie. This convinced me that I did want to be her daughter.

*   *   *

"Mia, I am glad you chose me as your mother. Now you need to let me tell my part of the story."

"Okay, Mom."

*   *   *

Francesca

Mia knows me as Mom, and she already told you my first name. My full name is Francesca Allen Lung. I will be telling you my part of this story.

As Mia said, I have always loved my family and my pets. I especially loved my horses and my dogs. Dad always said that he could not sell a horse if I was around. I would cry at the thought of losing my beloved pet. Dad used to say that I would make him go broke if he allowed me to keep every stray animal that wandered into my life. Yet my dad, a six-foot-two-inch, two-hundred-pound former marine, said I had him wrapped around my finger. He rarely refused me when I begged him to allow an animal to stay, at least until we could find it a home. I even saw him smile so big his dimples showed when we found good homes for puppies or kittens.

Still, I shed so many tears over the years over lost or dead animals. Dad was always there to pick up the pieces of my broken heart by enveloping me in his loving arms and gently patting my back. I still remember the feel of his chin resting on top of my head as he let me cry.

*   *   *

"This was just another example of how kindhearted you were, Mom. That is why I waited patiently for you to grow up. During this time, my love for you grew as I saw that you would one day be a loving and caring mother.

"When you were fifteen, I observed you playing tag football with all of your cousins. I noticed how protective you were of Angie and also of your younger cousins. I saw you run slowly when they were on the opposing team, allowing them to catch you. Then, I saw you cheer when they made a touchdown.

"I also observed how protective your big brother, George, was of all of you. He was the referee on the sideline, but when he thought you were in

6

danger, he called out to you, 'Francesca watch out!' then he dashed into the game to block a hard tackle from your brother, Paul, the one who was built like a linebacker. I heard him yell at Paul, 'Are you insane? Don't you know you could have really hurt her? What were you thinking?'

"Paul sulked for a few seconds before it dawned on him that George was right, so he got up and apologized to you.

"Your big sister Brenda ran over to make sure you were all okay before she said, 'Paul, you need to be more careful. This is supposed to be tag football, not tackle. Francesca could have really gotten hurt. You're twice her size.'

"You just said, 'Okay, you've both made Paul feel bad enough, and I'm fine. Can we get back to the game now?'"

"I watched you go on your first date when you were sixteen. I knew that at that time in your life, you only wanted to date, not settle down. Still, I remember seeing tears in Grandpa's eyes when he saw you drive away."

"You were right about how I felt. I didn't know Dad had such a hard time with my dating. He hid it well. When my first boyfriend said, 'I love you,' I said good-bye. You see, I was determined to have a career."

"Mom, Great-Grandma Laura told me that she put this idea in your head."

"Yes, Mia. Grandma Laura was the one who convinced me to have a career. An aunt, whom I loved very much, convinced me to become a physical therapist, even though science wasn't my best subject. My teachers actually tried to convince me to major in journalism, but my love for my aunt won in the end. Frankly, I was a little scared that I would not be successful as a journalist. Mia, now you know where your confidence problem comes from."

*   *   *

Francesca
While I was studying to be a physical therapist, I met the man I thought would one day be Mia's father. We dated off and on for two years. Every time I thought he had vanished from my life, he would reappear. Mia's grandmother would have said that he turned up like a bad penny. Because I saw him as my first real love, I always took him back. Now I know that this relationship was not healthy. Unfortunately, I did not see this at the time.

Finally, after two years of this, I called home in tears one night. Angie answered the phone on the third ring. Between sobs, I asked, "Angie, is Mom home?"

"No, she and Dad went to a Shriner's dance tonight," Angie said. "It's not like you to forget that. What's wrong?"

"It's so awful," I cried between sniffs and nose blowing. "Don is getting married, but he keeps calling me. Why can't he just leave me alone? I need help to get him completely out of my life."

"When Paul arrives on Friday, do you want me to ask him to get George to come down there with him to beat Don up?" Angie asked. "Just say the word, and I know our brothers will come to your rescue."

"I love the idea, but I know he isn't worth it. Besides, Brenda would beat me up if I let the boys handle my battles," I said as I wiped my tears.

Angie chuckled and said, "You're right about that. I can hear her now, 'Frankie, women are equal to men. Don't you dare let the boys fight your battles! Remember the pen is mightier than the sword, and lawyers are mightier than anyone. If you need help getting rid of the creep, I'll make some phone calls, and we'll get a bench warrant issued for harassment.'"

Brenda was a tough attorney, yet she also had a soft side where her family was concerned. She was the only one to ever call me Frankie.

After the laughter died away, in the softest, most soothing voice, my little sister gave me words of wisdom. "He is bad news. You know that. You deserve so much better. God pity his fiancée! You have to just hang up when he calls. You're coming home this weekend, right?"

As I wiped my nose, I said, "Of course, isn't this the weekend Paul is bringing Ann home?"

"Yes, it is. Brenda and Brad are having a family dinner for them on Saturday. Ann needs our support because she is a little overwhelmed at the thought of our large family gatherings since she is an only child."

"Has Paul proposed?" I asked.

Angie said, "Not officially. They're going to visit her parents the weekend after next. You know how old-fashioned Paul is. I think he plans to ask Ann's dad for her hand in marriage before he asks her."

"Why can't I find a guy like our brother?" I asked as I blew my nose again.

"Because you're too busy being hung up on heartbreakers like Don," Angie said before reminding me that our sister-in-law, Cindy, had offered to introduce me to a colleague of hers.

"Yes, but George even said he is not sure about that guy," I said as I threw away my wadded-up tissue.

"You and I both know George would never believe anyone was good enough for either of his little sisters," Angie said. "Besides, it sounds like you're looking for an excuse to avoid meeting someone new."

"You've got me on that one," I said as I looked at the clock and gasped. "I just realized it's ten o'clock already. I've got a test in the morning. I've got to get to bed, and you do too. I'll see you this weekend."

"Just promise me to avoid the jerk until then," Angie said.

"I promise," I said. "Good night."

"Good night," Angie said just before I heard the soft click of her hanging up.

With my family's love and support, I survived the break-up, but I no longer trusted my judgment.

*　　*　　*

"I was worried about you for a while, but Great-Grandma Laura told me that with the love and support of family, you would eventually realize you were lucky to be rid of Don. I certainly could feel the love of your family. It made me want to be a part of it too."

*　　*　　*

Francesca

A year later, I met Tim Ridge. He was from a good family, but he had many problems. We had been dating for two years when he moved to Whitefish, Montana. We broke up after he moved, but later, he called me to say that he realized that I was the most important person in his life. He begged me to follow him to Montana. I initially refused, but I did agree to visit him.

The moment I got off the plane, I fell in love with the Rocky Mountains. The plane landed just as the sun was disappearing behind the mountains. At dusk, the mountains really looked purple as in "purple mountain majesties."

*　　*　　*

"Yeah, you loved those mountains more than you loved Tim!"

"Mia, I know that's what you think. Maybe you're right, but I did care about him. I also really loved his family, especially his parents and grandparents. They stayed in touch with me even when Tim and I broke up."

*　　*　　*

Francesca

This was the longest I had been involved in a continuous relationship. I decided that this must mean we really loved each other, so after I received my master's degree in physical therapy from Western Carolina University, I moved to Montana to be with Tim. Still, we did not marry for another year. I guess both of us had doubts about our relationship. After a year, we agreed that it was time to decide whether we should make our relationship permanent.

If we had been honest, we would have admitted that while we were close friends, our love was not strong enough for marriage. Unfortunately, we were not honest, so we got married.

Initially, it seemed that our marriage would work. After all, we had started out as friends. However, Tim continued to pursue the party lifestyle while I started pursuing my career dreams. After three years of marriage, we grew apart, and I finally grew up, so I filed for divorce.

Three months after the divorce was final, Angie graduated from Colorado State University with a master's degree in occupational therapy. When the graduation was over, I rode with Angie to her graduation party at the home she and her roommates rented.

As she drove, she said, "Francesca ..." but then her voice caught. I could not tell whether it was from excitement or fear. "I've been offered a job with the Kalispell Home Health Agency." She grinned. "It's in Montana near Whitefish! If I take the job, can I live with you for a while? I will be studying for my boards the first couple of months, so I shouldn't be too much trouble."

I laughed. "Of course you can. I could use some help with expenses, and it would be so nice to have you as a roommate. We can go hiking together in the summer and skiing in the winter. It'll be great!"

Two weeks later, Angie moved in—and she brought her opinions with her. She told me she thought I should start dating again. She insisted that I have a housewarming party.

I supposed maybe she was right. Ever since I had moved into my condominium, right after my divorce, I had spent so much time working and sorting through all of the issues I'd had with past relationships that I hadn't even had any of my friends over.

So I finally agreed to the party. Angie said that she had some friends that she would like to invite too. This is how I met Mia's father, Benjamin Lung. Angie's boyfriend, Dave Lindell, knew him and asked if he could bring him to the party. We were inviting other single friends, so I said, "Why not?" Little did I know that this decision would change my life forever!

When Ben arrived, Angie introduced us. There was a sense of recognition along with a giddiness that I could not explain. I wanted to run away. Yet, how could anyone run away from such gorgeous, sparkling dark eyes? When he smiled, his entire face seemed to glow. I was imagining how it would feel to rest my head on his shoulder as I could see that he was the perfect height for me. I felt the world disappear around us for what seemed like minutes, when in fact, it couldn't have been more than a few seconds. It was love at first sight, and I was terrified!

I really was not ready for a relationship. I still had to figure out why I had been attracted to the wrong men in my previous relationships. Still, we spent most of the evening talking to each other. I learned that he had become a pediatrician because he loved kids. He had taken a job in Montana as a way to repay some of his debt. Doctors could work in rural settings for a period of time in exchange for having some of their debt eliminated.

He had learned to cross-country ski, and he enjoyed hiking, so he spent time in the nearby national park every chance he got. He was definitely my type of guy! His family was very important to him, so he was planning to move back to Hawaii, his home state, once he fulfilled his obligation. He had only one more year to work in Montana.

I decided that since Ben would be moving away, I did not have to worry about him, which was a big relief. I had already decided that I was not ready to date. This solved the problem. Ben would be back in Hawaii before I was even ready to look seriously at a man again.

The next day, the phone rang. Angie answered it. "It's for you," she said as she handed me the phone.

"Hello, Francesca. This is Ben. I was wondering if you would like to go hiking with me tomorrow. We could pick up some deli sandwiches and have a picnic lunch."

"That sounds nice," I said surprising myself.

After that, Ben and I were together every weekend. I was still afraid to trust my heart. Ben was also cautious, as he had never been in a serious relationship because he had been too busy earning his medical degree and then completing his specialty training.

Ben moved back to Hawaii, and we had a long-distance relationship for almost three years. Poor Angie was my sounding board as I kept trying to come up with reasons why this relationship would not work. His mother disapproved of me because I was not Chinese. We came from two different cultures. If I married him and moved to Hawaii, I would be far away from my family. Last but certainly not least, I loved Montana. I was a mountain person, not a beach person.

Angie persisted in telling me again and again, "As long as you and Ben continue to have mutual love and respect for each other, nothing can come between you. I know you believe this too."

Love and respect were two things I knew I could count on Ben to give. This gave me confidence that we would be able to overcome any obstacles as long as we supported each other. Ben and I finally learned to trust our hearts and planned our wedding.

Despite the love we shared, the move to Hawaii after the wedding was not easy for me. I really loved the Rockies, and I had spent most of my weekends in the mountains. I missed this, and I really missed Angie. Also, I had left many close friends behind.

*   *   *

"Mom, I know leaving Montana was hard for you. I saw how much you loved the mountains. I watched you go cross-country skiing in the spring before you married Dad. I could tell that you were telling the mountains good-bye. I saw how sad it made you. I do not really think that Dad understood at the time."

"It wasn't your Dad's fault. He really didn't understand. He'd never felt that kind of love for a place where he did not grow up. Of course, he did know that I'd miss Angie. He just assumed that since I had already moved away from my family that the move would be easy for me."

*   *   *

Francesca
It wasn't! Hawaii was somewhat of a culture shock. You see, in Hawaii, people would always ask you which high school you attended. This seemed to matter more than where you went to college. They really just wanted to know, "How are you connected to this rock (island)?"

Because many of the people had known each other since kindergarten, I found it hard to make close friends. In some ways, it was even harder because I was married to Ben. You see, I was a down-to-earth type of person, and most people assumed that a doctor's wife would not be.

I had always had lots of friends, ranging from grocery clerks to professionals. My friends in Montana knew me before I married. They knew that I would not change just because I had married a doctor. The people in Hawaii, however, had not known me before, so they did not know this.

To make matters worse, Ben had graduated from a prestigious private school, so most people assumed he was snobby. While he appeared that way at times, Ben was not a snob. I would never have married a snob!

Ben was also used to the Asian culture, as he had grown up in Hawaii and was Chinese American. Because he loved me and because I had Asian friends, he just assumed I would fully understand the culture. He belonged, while I did not. This was very hard for me. I always felt like I belonged in Montana. I was so homesick for my adopted home state!

In Hawaii, I was (and still am) a *haole*, a foreigner or white person, who did not understand why which high school a person attended was so important or many other things that people who grew up in Hawaii took for granted. At least I did eat the local foods. Two of my close friends in Montana were of Japanese descent. One of them was actually married to a boy from the Big Island (the island of Hawaii). The other friend had lived in Hawaii.

They were both supportive during this time. If only I had fully understood the far-reaching effects of the move at the time!

*   *   *

"Mom, this is where I entered the scene. After living in Hawaii for almost a year, you were just beginning to make friends at work and starting to learn your way around the island. You had joined professional organizations, and you were active on committees. Then you found out that you were pregnant. The timing was awful!"

"Mia, I know that you think that you complicated my life. Maybe you did later; however, not when I found out that I was pregnant with you. Your dad and I were very happy then."

"I wonder if you would have been as happy if you had known just how much I was going to change your lives. Mom, I know you would probably say yes, but there must have been times when you wondered this too."

"Yes, Mia, I would definitely say yes. Two of the greatest joys in my life were when I found out that I was pregnant with you and the day that you were born."

*   *   *

Ben did not get to go with me to the appointment at which I found out that I was pregnant. I was extremely happy and could not wait to tell him. I tried calling him on my cell phone from the hospital parking lot. He was busy with a patient at the time, so I had to wait for him to call me back. The wait seemed to last for ages. When I finally reached Ben, he was as excited as I was. We went to get a book of names that evening and soon had the right name picked out: Mia.

I called Angie the next day to tell her the news. I heard a squeal before she said, "You know we have to go shopping for maternity clothes when you visit, right? I can't believe you'll be here in two weeks!"

We had already planned a trip to Denver. Angie and Dave had moved there four months after our wedding so she could work on her doctorate. The rest of my family was coming to Denver the following week to celebrate Thanksgiving. It would be the first time that we would all be together since our wedding.

The doctor insisted that I have an ultrasound the week before the trip to ensure that Mia was okay. I was so excited to see the heartbeat. Ben could not make it to the ultrasound, so I had the doctor give me a picture to show him. This was Mia's first picture.

The next week, Angie and Dave met us at the baggage claim area of

Denver International Airport. Angie was almost jumping with excitement as she waved her left hand in front of me. "Francesca, look! Dave and I are getting married."

I reached for her hand and saw a beautiful emerald and diamond ring. "Wow! The ring is gorgeous. I am so happy for both of you! Have you set a date yet?" I asked as I gave her a big hug.

Then as I reached over to hug Dave, he said, "Before you two get into the details of this conversation, I think we should grab your luggage and head to the parking lot so we can avoid rush-hour traffic."

Ben pulled our last bag off the carousel as he said, "Congratulations, you two! Dave, I agree with you." He turned to me and said, "You two can catch up on the way to their house."

As we walked out of the airport, Angie said, "We haven't set the exact date yet, but we're thinking about sometime around Christmas next year. That way, my little niece or nephew will be six months old already so you can travel. I want you to be my matron of honor."

As we arrived at their car, I put my carry-on down to hug my sister again as I said, "Of course, I'll be your matron of honor. There is just one problem. How will we know my dress size? How will I be able to get it fitted in time?"

Both of our guys looked at each other and shook their heads. Dave said, "I think you should ride up front with me so these two can discuss wedding plans."

Angie said, "Good idea! I'll sit behind Dave so Ben can still be included in our conversation. Now where were we? Oh yeah, you had concerns about getting your dress fitted. I've already talked to the bridal shop. I explained that you're pregnant and that you'll still be nursing your baby at the time of the wedding. They have some ideas for dresses that might work. You won't need to do the final fitting here. We can send the dress to you. The final fitting can be done in Hawaii."

Angie tapped Ben on the shoulder and asked, "Ben, what do you think? After all, it'll be the baby's first Christmas. Will you be able to take time off from work? Do you think that your family would be willing to travel here to celebrate Christmas?"

Ben looked over his left shoulder as he said, "I think I can manage to get away at Christmas. Most of my patients travel then anyway. Francesca and I already talked about spending the baby's first Christmas with your parents. At least traveling to Colorado is not as far. I'm almost sure that I can talk Mom, Dad, and Kevin into coming to Colorado for Christmas. I'll have to ask Lester and Diane, but you have my vote." (Kevin and Lester were Ben's younger brothers. Diane was his sister-in-law.)

"Thanks, guys. You're the best. Now I just have to convince the rest of our family. Mom and Dad are the only ones we've told so far."

As the car pulled into their garage, Dave said, "We're home. I'll get your luggage while Angie gives you the grand tour."

I loved Angie and Dave's house. They had a two-story, four-bedroom, and three-and-a-half-bathroom home with a three-car garage in Westminster, a northwestern suburb of Denver.

The kitchen was the last room on Angie's tour. It had a large round table beside a sliding glass door that faced a huge backyard. I could see the mountains in the background. Dave met us there with hot chocolate. As we sat around the kitchen table sipping our warm drinks, Angie explained that she was so glad that Dave had gotten the hospital administrator job at St. Anthony North, as being on the north side of town made her commute to Fort Collins for school so much easier.

As we finished our hot chocolate, Angie asked, "Francesca, how are you feeling? Do you feel well enough to go shopping? I want to help you pick out some maternity clothes before I drag you to the wedding shop to help me decide on a dress. I know it's early, but I want my sister to help me pick my wedding dress, and I know you won't be traveling again until after the baby is born."

I said, "I feel fine, but I bet Ben isn't going to want to go shopping."

Angie laughed. "Ben and Dave aren't invited. They're on their own." She turned to the guys and waved as she said, "We'll see you later."

I was excited to find that the maternity store had pillows that allowed me to see what I would look like as Mia grew. Angie had her camera, and she made me model as she snapped multiple pictures. Ben said that I almost broke the bank that day. I came home with more clothes than I had ever bought at one time.

Angie and I also had the best time picking out her wedding dress and my matron of honor dress. It was my turn to borrow Angie's camera to take pictures of her as she posed. We also had the lady helping us take pictures of the two of us together. It was definitely an exciting time!

The rest of my family arrived the next week, and our time together flew by too quickly. While Mom and Dad had aged in the last year, they actually looked distinguished. Mom was of average height, but beside Dad's six feet two inches, she always looked small. They were both in their mid-sixties. Mom still had auburn hair, but she had more gray around her temples. It complemented her hazel eyes, which sometimes appeared gray. She had more laugh lines around her mouth. Dad's hair was completely white, which made his emerald-green eyes stand out more, but he seemed to be having trouble with shortness of breath, although he assured Angie that he would be able to walk her down the aisle. (Our father had lung cancer five years earlier, but he had a lobectomy and they were sure they had gotten it all. He was currently in remission.)

Angie and Dave had a houseful of people for Thanksgiving. Our oldest sibling, George, who looked more and more like a younger version of Dad complete with golden blond hair and dimples, came with his wife, Cindy, who was a pretty, brown-eyed brunette, and their two kids, four-year-old Lisa, who was looking more and more like her mom, and two-year-old Adam, who looked like his dad and grandpa. Then our older sister, Brenda, who could have been Mom's twin if there hadn't been twenty-six years' difference in their ages, arrived with her redheaded husband, Brad, and their six-month-old, Jenny, who, of course, looked like her mom and grandma. Last to arrive was our brother, Paul, our six-feet-four-inch, red-haired warrior, who was still built like a linebacker, and his still adorable, redheaded wife Ann. It was good to see all of them.

Before I knew it, we had to return to Hawaii. As we prepared to board the plane, I was thinking how much I already missed Angie. I had laughed so much during the two weeks we spent in Denver.

Because I would turn thirty-five a week before Mia was born, my doctor wanted me to have an amniocentesis to make sure Mia was okay. It was scheduled for the middle of January. As the time approached, I really was wishing Angie was there.

* * *

"Mom, I remember that test. I wanted you to see how smart I was so I had my hand on the side of my head with my fingers moving so I looked like I was thinking about something. This also gave you more time to see me. The doctor had to wait for me to move my hand before he could measure my brain."

"Mia, getting to see you for so long made the procedure worthwhile. Of course, I was also glad a few weeks later when I found out you were okay and that you were a girl."

* * *

Francesca
I would not see Mia again until she was born. In the meantime, I talked to her and played music for her while I waited for her to arrive.

Mia thinks this was when she first fell in love with classical music and with Celine Dion. My favorite song at the time was "The Power of Love."

Mia always hit and kicked my belly in response to the music. She also hit and kicked our dog, Lightning, when he sat in front of me. I thought they were bonding.

Mia

I think I was actually a little jealous of him. He was Mom's first baby. Dad got to feel my punches and kicks sometimes too. His hands felt strong when I hit or kicked them.

Listening to my mom, I decided that I wanted to be born sooner, so when Mom was thirty-two weeks into her pregnancy, I tried to start her labor by kicking her repeatedly. Mom had contractions and slight dilation from this, but the doctor said it was too early for my birth, so he put my mom on bed rest and terbutaline.

Francesca

The last weeks before Mia was born were especially difficult. The terbutaline made me jittery. Also, I hated being on bed rest, as I had been active prior to this. I even walked every day and did modified aerobics during my pregnancy.

On top of dealing with the complications of pregnancy, I was dealing with housing contractors. We were trying to finish remodeling our house so it would be perfect by the time Mia was born. The construction was supposed to have been finished two months before I started bed rest. Unfortunately, everything moves at a slower pace in Hawaii, including construction work.

We were staying with my in-laws because of the construction. I could tell my mother-in-law was just as uncomfortable with my being in her house as I was. I actually stayed at work as long as possible every day to avoid going home.

I was sleeping on a cot in Ben's old room while he was sleeping in his old twin bed. The cot was very uncomfortable. Finally, Ben realized how uncomfortable I was and switched beds with me. His mother asked him what was wrong with the cot when she found out. She said it was a new cot and she was sure it was fine. Ben told her that the mattress was thin and that it wasn't comfortable even for him. His mom got upset with him when he told her this. This made things harder for all of us. I told Ben that I needed to be back in my own bed if I had to be on bed rest.

Ben talked to the construction workers and managed to get them to finish our bedroom and bathroom as quickly as possible. Luckily, the kitchen was already completed. We were able to move back home during my first week of bed rest.

Of course, the contractors and builders were at the house every day trying to complete the rest of the house. They tried not to bother me, but questions came up at least daily. While the contractors knew that I was on bed rest, the carpet installers, burglar alarm installers, and the cable company installers did not.

My in-laws left on a trip to the mainland a couple of weeks after I started bed rest, so they were not around to help. That was okay since, honestly, I probably would not have wanted their help anyway.

I wanted my own mom or one of my sisters, but they were too far away. Angie actually offered to come, but she was still in school and I knew that she was also busy with her wedding plans. My mom would have come, but I knew that she and Dad were not doing as well as they pretended because Brenda had told me that Dad still had shortness of breath sometimes. They were also busy making plans for Angie's wedding, and I did not want to spoil it. Brenda had her own family to take care of, and she also had her career to manage.

I really missed talking to Mom and Dad about how I felt. My dad was always my sounding board for any of life's major decisions. I did not always follow his advice, but I always listened to him. Even though I had been away from home for years, I knew my dad was always there for me. Anytime I needed him, all I had to do was call.

Still, I didn't call them this time. I did not want to hear, "Sweetheart, I'm so sorry. I did try to warn you that things might be difficult, especially with your being so far from home."

To make matters worse, I also had severe heartburn, which prevented me from getting much sleep at night. My greatest fear was that the contractor would not complete the house before Mia was born. I was grumpy with everyone.

Mia
That's an understatement! I had never seen my Mom so mad.

Only our dog, Lightning, seemed to make her happy. He was her constant companion during this time.

Frankly, I was a little jealous of how much she loved him. I had to remind myself this love of animals would make her a great mom.

Francesca
Finally, I was far enough into my pregnancy to stop the terbutaline. This was Mia's cue.

Chapter III
Birth, Family, Subtle Signs

Mia

I decided to wait a little longer to be born. I had noticed Mom's anxiety about the house, so I waited until it was finished. Finally, the day after the house was finished, I woke Mom up at 7:30 AM. I was in a hurry to see her.

Francesca

The day of Mia's birth, I woke up with contractions, but I let Ben sleep until 9:00, as I wanted to make sure that I was not having false labor. When he got up, I refused to call the doctor right away. I did not want to go to the hospital too soon. I was afraid they would send us back home. I cooked and ate a light breakfast and took a shower and then watched some TV. I finally called my doctor, who suggested that I go to the hospital once my contractions were three minutes apart. I told him that they were already three minutes apart. He told me to go straight to the hospital. By the time we got to the hospital, it was 1:00 PM. Mia was born four hours later. I avoided taking any medication so Mia was born wide awake.

Mia

My dad's face greeted me as I entered the world. He was the one to cut my umbilical cord. It was great to meet Dad. However, I really could not wait to see Mom. I was so excited! When I finally was face-to-face with Mom, I kept looking at her.

Ah Ma and Ah Gung were back from the mainland. They arrived at the hospital shortly after I was born. Ah Ma wanted to hold me the whole time. She seemed to be keeping me away from Mom. While Ah Ma seemed nice, I really just wanted my mom.

Francesca

I was so happy to see Mia finally! I had been trying to imagine what she would look like. She was beautiful. She had Ben's full head of jet black hair with alert dark eyes that kept looking straight at me even when my mother-in-law held her. I wanted her back, but I knew she needed to bond with her grandparents too.

Ben must have realized that I needed to hold her longer because he said, "Mom, Francesca hasn't had much time with Mia because they were weighing and measuring her. I think she would like to hold her again."

My mother-in-law reluctantly gave Mia to me. Then she turned to the nurse and asked if she could have the blood pressure cuff and the measuring tape they used to check Mia. They told her that it would all go home with Mia.

I sighed and smiled at this. For once, my mother-in-law wasn't the one in charge.

I did rooming in, so that I could have more time with my daughter. Ben spent the afternoon and most of the evening with us, but he went home that night to sleep. He even went to work the next day. He came back again right after work. Then he took off to be with us when we first came home from the hospital the following day.

Mia

My first day home, I met Lightning, our German shepherd. He and I became close friends, although he kept trying to steal the show every time my parents took pictures of me. He was in most of my baby pictures. Luckily, he was a mature, gentle soul. I know that he would not have tolerated me so well otherwise.

I also spent more quality time with Dad, as now he could hold me and talk to me directly. I think we loved each other very much then, although we would both question this love later.

Dad's parents were also a part of my life. Ah Ma would hold me every chance she got. She sometimes smelled of garlic and ginger, her two favorite spices. Her hair felt rougher than Mom's when it touched my face, as she bent to kiss me. Her voice was higher pitched than normal when she spoke to me.

Ah Gung held me too, but his voice was much softer. I did not know what his hair felt like because he never kissed me, and his black hair was too short to have touched my face anyway. He sometimes smelled of barbeque smoke because he liked to grill. I don't think he was comfortable holding me, as he was always giving me back to Mom. I think that he thought that I would break. Dads of his generation were not hands-on when it came to caring for their babies.

Soon, I met my Uncle Kevin, Dad's little brother. He had thick black hair and looked similar to my dad but was slightly taller. He smelled of sunshine and sea breezes. He was still single when I was born, so he still lived with Ah Ma and Ah Gung. (In Hawaii, many young adults live with their parents because it is too hard to afford an apartment on one income because of the high cost of living.) He had been on a trip when I was born, so I did not meet him until I was two weeks old.

Uncle Kevin was so sweet. He told me funny stories, and then he would say, "Mia, I know you got the punch line, but you're just too young to smile, so I'll smile for both of us." Uncle Kevin was our family entrepreneur. He sold sports equipment that he designed. He was also a poet. I really liked him.

I would not get to meet Mom's parents until I was six months old. They were getting older and were busy helping plan Auntie Angie's wedding. Mom assured them that I would meet them at the wedding, and they sent me my first teddy bear, a cute, dark pink bear named Teddy who became my protector. Mom sent videos and pictures of me, including ones of me with Teddy, to my grandparents.

When they would call, Mom would put the phone to my ear so I could hear their voices. Mom's family talked differently than my other relatives. I would later learn that they had Southern accents. I decided that I loved their voices, as they sounded warm and loving. They said, "I love you very much, and I can't wait to see you. We love the pictures and videos your mom sends us. We're so glad you like Teddy. Think of us and how much we love you when you play with her." I could feel the love through the phone. Plus, Mom was so relaxed when she talked to them.

My mom stopped working after I was born so she could take care of me. We spent all of our time together, which I loved. She made everything fun.

We went grocery shopping together. Mom told me the name of everything she put into our basket. For fruits and vegetables, she also told me their color.

When Mom cooked, she would put my high chair in the kitchen and let me have my own pot and spoon to pretend to cook too.

We took Lightning out to run together. Okay, technically, I rode in the jogging stroller, but as I grew, I reached for his leash. He was so good; he slowed down when I did this. I really loved the feel of the trade winds on my face as Mom ran. Mom pointed out yellow and red hibiscus and yellow and pink plumerias along our route, and if a flower was on the ground, she would sometimes pick it up for me to feel and hold. Once we saw a man trimming a palm tree. The man was so high up that Mom had to turn back the stroller canopy for me to see. He was strapped to the tree with a wide belt, and he was removing the coconuts and placing them in a big bag around his shoulder. He climbed down so fast it was scary. I turned away because I thought he would fall, but Mom told me to look because the man was already safely on the ground.

We had picnics in our backyard and at the park. Okay, you caught me again, I was too young to eat yet, but I did lie on a blanket that Mom spread out over a beach mat. Mom let ladybugs land on her finger so she could show me. She also pointed out geckos to me, but even with a cute name, lizards were not cute to me. She also pointed to birds and told me what type they were. We frequently saw Japanese white-eyes, small green birds with white eyes, who liked to land on the huge aloe vera plants in our backyard; myna birds, who squawked loudly; mountain doves, big birds with a lace-collar pattern around their necks; and zebra doves, smaller doves with no collars.

We did aerobics together and lifted weights together. Okay, I'm busted again. I did not do this initially, but I watched.

Francesca
When Mia was just five months old, I found two water bottles shaped like weights. Mia used these to pretend to lift weights when I did my exercises.

I tried to include Mia in all aspects of my life, so I introduced her to books when she was only two weeks old. I have always loved to read, and I wanted her to grow up loving books.

I read at least one book to her during the day, and I always read her a bedtime story too, so by the time she was six months old, she was already pretending to read her books while I read mine.

Mia
My favorite time was bedtime. My mom would hold me while she read my favorite story, and she would let me turn the pages. Then she would sing to me as we rocked together in the rocking chair.

* * *

"Mia, this was my favorite time too. I loved how you smelled like baby shampoo after your bath and how soft your skin was as I held you."

* * *

Mia
My dad spent all of his time with us in the evenings and on weekends. We went shopping and out to dinner at least once a week. We even went to the

beach occasionally with Uncle Kevin, although neither of my parents really liked the beach much and, frankly, I didn't either. I hated touching the sand. It wasn't just that it was hot; it actually caused pain similar to that of a paper cut on my skin when I touched it.

I had other subtle differences from other babies from the start. I was obsessed with the spin toy in my crib. I learned to spin it myself when I was only six weeks old. Mom also caught me pulling the crib mirror away from the side of the crib. I looked behind it and then looked at the front of the mirror again.

*   *   *

"Mia, this is when I figured out how smart you are. I probably should have been worried!"

*   *   *

Mia

I was different in other ways too. If I spilled a teaspoon of water on my clothes, I cried until my clothes where changed, but not because I was cold—after all, I lived in Hawaii and it was usually 85 degrees outside.

I also had to have Teddy, my pink bear, strapped in my car seat and even in the stroller with me. She protected me from the strange world when we went places. When Mom rushed out the door without her, I cried and cried until Mom had to go back to get her. I needed her until I quit using the stroller when I was two and a half.

*   *   *

"Sensory issues could explain many of your differences, including not wanting to wear a shirt that had a tiny wet spot. Even using Teddy to protect you from the outside world and your obsession with the spin toy may have been related to undiagnosed sensory sensitivity and Asperger's syndrome. We didn't realize any of this was abnormal at the time."

*   *   *

Mia

When I was six months old, we flew to Denver for Auntie Angie's wedding. This was when I finally met my maternal grandparents. We flew all night. I did not sleep at all on the plane. My parents even gave me Benadryl, but it did not work. Luckily, I did not cry much during the flight despite not sleeping.

Francesca

We now know how strange this was! At the time, we just assumed that Mia was having a reaction to the Benadryl that caused her to be hyper. It was actually because of sensory issues and trouble with changes in her routine, but since we weren't aware of these issues at the time, we just attributed it to the Benadryl.

Because she did not sleep, the trip to Denver was awful. When we flew together before Mia was born, I usually took catnaps and read on the plane. Ben usually just napped. Now one of us had to try to entertain her. We were worried that she would disturb the other passengers. We were thanking God that she did not cry much.

Ben and I were exhausted when we finally arrived at Angie's house. We arrived a week before the wedding, and we were thankful there were no events planned. Mom and Dad were already there, and they had everything under control. I told them, "All three of us really need to catch up on our sleep. Mia stayed awake the whole way here."

"Of course," Angie said. "Go take a nap. Sleep as long as you need. If Mia wakes up before you, I'll watch her."

Mom said, "We will watch Mia. Angie still has wedding things to do, and we need to get to know our granddaughter."

I smiled at my wonderful family. Then I interjected a little reality check. "She needs to get used to all of you before you start fighting over who's going to watch her. Angie, are we in the same room as last time, and did you manage to borrow a crib?"

"Yes and yes. There are towels on the bed if you want to shower."

"Okay, thanks. I need to feed Mia and get her down for her nap first."

Ben said, "I'll shower while you do that."

Mia

At my auntie's house, I saw Mom's love for her family. I also saw their love for her. Grandma and Grandpa insisted that we sleep late in the mornings. They knew we were still on Hawaii time. They even stayed up late with us in the evenings.

Francesca

Dad and Mom were wonderful. They understood that allowances needed to be made for the three-hour time difference. They knew Mia needed downtime, not just nap time. I had missed them so much. Dad's skin color seemed off, and he was still slightly short of breath. Yet, he bounced Mia on his knee. He was amazing.

Mia

I met my aunts, uncles, and cousins a couple of days later. Melanie, my Uncle Paul and Auntie Ann's daughter, was the cousin closest to my age. She was just a month younger than I was. We didn't look like cousins because she had red hair and pretty blue eyes like both of her parents. We played together on a big rug on the kitchen floor while the adults were busy talking and our other cousins were off somewhere. Of course, at this stage of life, playing for me meant grabbing the toy the fastest so she could not get it.

All of our aunties and uncles wanted to hold Melanie and me. Of course, they already knew her because she lived in the South too. She did not cry when they held her, as I sometimes did. Being passed from person to person would put me in sensory overload, especially if they spoke too loudly or if they tried to get me to interact with them the very first time I saw them. No one knew this; everyone just thought it was because I was a shy kid who didn't know them well yet.

Still, I loved all of my aunties: Auntie Brenda, Auntie Angie, Auntie Cindy, and Auntie Ann. They all held me gently and spoke softly to me. My uncles were a little too rough initially. Once they learned this scared me, they too became gentler and spoke more softly to me.

I eventually got used to all of the adults in Mom's family. I really loved Grandpa and Grandma because they were so much fun. Grandpa bounced me on his knee as he made clicking sounds so I could pretend I was riding a prancing horse, and Grandma sang "Twinkle, Twinkle, Little Star" and "You Are My Sunshine" to me. They both told me that they loved seeing me smile. Grandpa said my smile reminded him of Mom when she was little. Grandma told me how much she loved the cute pink sweatshirts and my pretty pink coat. She said pink was her favorite color. It became mine too.

They had invited all of their friends to Auntie Angie's wedding. Grandpa and Grandma kept introducing me to them. They kept saying to their friends, "Did you meet our beautiful, exotic granddaughter? All of our grandkids are truly grand."

Ah Ma, Ah Gung, and Uncle Kevin came two days before Christmas. They were staying until after the wedding. Ah Ma would go with us to visit Uncle Lester and Auntie Diane when we left Colorado. Ah Gung and Uncle Kevin would return to Hawaii.

Francesca

While Mia was taking an early afternoon nap on Christmas Eve, a light snow began to fall. I was sitting in the kitchen with Ben and Dad. I said, "I really want to go for a walk to feel the snow again. I miss it."

Dad said, "I'll go with you. I need to stretch my legs; plus, I want to talk to you about something."

Ben said, "You two go. I'll be here if Mia wakes up."

So Dad and I grabbed our coats and borrowed snow boots, hats, and gloves from Dave and Angie and took a walk. It was so nice to feel the wonderful dry snowflakes hit my eyelashes. I know it may sound strange, but I had missed snow so much. I didn't even mind that I needed to walk slower than normal for Dad's sake. I was just enjoying the moment and also Dad's company. Dad must have sensed this, because he didn't say anything until we had walked six blocks. Then I noticed tears in his eyes as he put his hand on my shoulder and said, "I need to talk to you. I had a checkup right before we came. That phone call I received this morning was from Dr. Johnson. The cancer has returned, and I don't want Angie to know until after the wedding."

"Can't you have more chemo or another surgery so you can fight this?" I cried as he pulled me toward him. My head was buried in his shoulder as he patted my shoulder.

"I will fight it again, but I already know how much trouble I have had breathing since the lobectomy. This time, they will need to remove what is left of my right lung. I have to undergo tests for metastasis when we get home. The outlook is not as hopeful this time.

"Remember, I don't want Angie to know. Please don't spoil her wedding. My biggest regret is that I will not live to see my grandchildren grow up and that I won't live to see any of Angie's children or any other grandchildren that you and Ben or Paul and Ann may have. I know that Mia and Melanie won't remember me."

I reached into my coat pocket to pull out a tissue. I passed one to Dad, and then I blotted my eyes with another. "Dad, Ben and I do want to have another child, but Paul and Ann told me that Melanie will be an only child. I promise you that my kids will know you through stories that I'll tell them. I'm sure Paul and Ann will tell Melanie about you as well. We'll all tell Angie's children about you. We're taking videos of you with Mia that will prove how much you love her."

I knew he was ill at the time; that is probably why I remember it so vividly even now. He only told me because he knew that he might not live to see me again.

Family surrounded Mia for her first Christmas. I could not have asked for anything more. We had asked everyone to keep any Christmas gifts small since we had to stop in California on the way home. Luckily, they listened to us. Mia's biggest gift was a guardian angel bear from her Ah Ma and Ah Gung. I couldn't believe they lugged it to Colorado instead of giving it to her in Hawaii. The best gift was having all of my family together and Mia being with both sides of her family for her first Christmas.

The wedding day was two days after Christmas. The bride was radiant in her wedding gown with ivory lace. She looked like an angel with her honey-colored hair flowing in front of her veil. Her blue eyes sparkled. Adam was such a cute ring bearer, and Lisa and Jenny were adorable flower girls, although Jenny was only seventeen months old and had to be carried most of the way by her mom. The rest of us were happy as well. Even though I was sad about my dad's illness, to this day, I still think of it as a happy time.

Two days after the wedding, it was time to leave for California. Mia still had to meet her Uncle Lester and Auntie Diane because they had not been able to make it to Colorado. Mia also had to meet Ben's grandmother and his aunties and uncles from his mom's side. It was hard to say good-bye to my parents. After my conversation with Dad, I really did not want to leave my family. I was so worried about him. Ben tried to keep Mia from seeing me cry as I said my good-byes.

Mia

I hated leaving Grandma and Grandpa. They had been so much fun. I waved good-bye to them after they hugged and kissed me. Then we boarded the plane. This flight was shorter than our previous flight, but it was scary. The plane seemed to rock at times. There was a lot more noise too because very few people slept. The flight attendants moved up and down the aisles with heavy carts that seemed to block us in our seats. I was in overload.

Ah Ma leaned forward from the seat behind us to ask Mom if she could take me. Mom told her that we were fine. Later, Mom let Ah Ma hold me part of the trip. I felt more secure in Mom's arms, as she just held me and softly kissed my head if I seemed startled. Ah Ma seemed to think she had to talk to me the whole time, which only made me feel more overwhelmed.

When I started to cry, Mom got up to get me. I was so grateful, but the trip was still awful. I really hated it, especially when my ears hurt as we were landing despite the fact that Mom gave me a bottle.

*　　*　　*

"Mia, I knew you were not happy on that flight, but I did not know that you were scared or that you hated it so much. At least it was a daytime flight and Ben and I had Ah Ma to help us. We all took turns looking after you and the time seemed to go quickly."

*　　*　　*

Francesca

When we arrived in California, Ben's brother, Lester, was waiting for us in his car outside of the baggage claim area. Once we were in the car heading toward his house, he announced that he and Diane had a big party planned for the next day. They had invited all of the California relatives, including Ben's grandmother, so Mia could meet them. I really did not feel like a party. Still, I knew Mia needed to meet her California relatives. I thanked Lester for planning this.

Mia

Because Uncle Lester was in a loading zone when he picked us up at the airport, I didn't really get to meet him officially until we got to his house. He didn't really look like Dad or Uncle Kevin. He resembled Ah Ma, differing only in having masculine features and a deeper voice—and he was taller of course. Auntie Diane had pretty wavy black hair and a soft voice. I probably would have liked her except I was still grumpy from the plane ride. I cried when either of them tried to hold me. They eventually just gave up.

The day after we arrived, their house was full of people. It was loud and a little scary. Everyone kept trying to hold me, and unlike Mom's family, they did not seem to understand that they needed to adjust the level of their voices or the way they held me. I would cry, and they would give me back to Mom or Dad. Mom and Dad insisted that I spend time with Tai Po (my Chinese great-grandmother) as they took pictures of the two of us together.

Tai Po reminded me of Ah Ma. Her voice had the same high-pitched tone. She spoke a strange language that I could not understand. Uncle Lester and Ah Ma told me what she said. Mom said that I had Tai Po's nose. This made Tai Po laugh. Then Tai Po gave me *lai see* (money in a red envelope). I did not know what it was for, but Uncle Lester and Dad said that it was a tradition for older relatives to give lucky money to younger relatives, especially on Chinese New Year.

Two days later, it was time to leave. Uncle Lester and Auntie Diane promised to come to Hawaii for a visit.

Chapter IV
TRANSITIONS

Francesca

When we got back home, it was somewhat lonely, but Mia and I soon settled back into our old routine. Mia would sometimes try to talk to my brothers and sisters when they called; other times, she just refused to talk. When Lester and Diane called, she rarely talked. Mia talked the most to Mom and Dad when they called, as she recognized their voices. She even tried to say Grandma and Grandpa. It sounded like "Grrrma" and "Grrrpa." They kept telling her how grown-up she sounded. This made Mia smile. She was always so happy when we talked to them.

During one call, six weeks after his surgery, they told me that Dad's tests all came back negative for further metastasis. He still had to do a course of chemotherapy and go for follow-up visits with the oncologist. I had wanted to visit soon after his surgery, but he insisted that it was too hard for me to travel by myself with Mia. He said that I should wait until Ben could take off again.

Mia

I blew kisses to Grandma and Grandpa on the videotapes that Mom made for them. I even told them, "Hi!" and "Love you!" on the tapes and when I talked to them on the phone. As I grew older, I talked more and sang for them on the tapes, but I still kept my phone conversations very short. Still, I felt their love for me. Plus, they wrote me long letters that Mom read to me.

*   *   *

"I could tell you loved your grandparents by the way you smiled when you talked about them and when I read their letters to you. Even choosing Teddy

29

as your protector showed how much they meant to you. What I didn't understand was why you wanted to get off the phone so fast when you talked to them.

"Mia, now we know that kids with Asperger's syndrome, especially those with sensory issues, do not usually like talking on the phone for very long. The phone against their ears may hurt or the volume may be too loud."

Mia

I started walking when I was ten months old. My parents tried to get me to go barefoot in our backyard. I cried and said, "Shoes, shoes."
Uncle Kevin still took me to the beach and tried to get me to go barefoot. When I refused, he picked me up and walked me to our beach mat. Then he tried to get me to play in the sand while sitting on the beach mat.

If Mom had known about my sensory issues, she would have seen that Uncle Kevin's ideas might have actually helped. He had the right idea of gradually trying to get me to increase my exposure to sand.

Eventually, Uncle Kevin gave up on helping me. He had other interests. He had started dating my future auntie, Renee. She was from the mainland. At the time, she was about to graduate from the University of Hawaii.

Francesca

Not wanting to walk barefoot on grass or sand is a symptom of Asperger's syndrome. If we had known that at the time, we might have been able to get Mia help with her sensory issues then. Even without knowing the signs, we should have recognized that this was a difference that would predict the future. After all, we lived in Hawaii, and most of our friends' kids refused to wear shoes until they were forced to when they started kindergarten. The only thing they ever wore on their feet when they were toddlers were rubber slippers (flip-flops).

Mia

I did not worry about losing Uncle Kevin. I was too busy exploring everything in my world. That was why my crib was too confining. I kept trying to climb out until one day, I succeeded.

*   *   *

"Mia, you were such an explorer. You were only fourteen months old when you climbed out of your crib. I was so afraid that you would fall and get hurt. I finally decided to get you a bed. I had you go with me to help pick it out. We looked at regular twin beds, but they were too high off the floor. Then one of our friends suggested a futon, so we went to the futon furniture store."

*   *   *

Mia

Right in the front of the store, I saw a white bed with a matching dresser. I pointed and said, "That one." I climbed in to make sure it was low enough. Then I climbed down and ran to the dresser. I opened one of the drawers and said, "Like Mommy's."

When Mom asked if I wanted to get it, I had a grin from ear to ear as I nodded. She told me that there would be more room for my stuffed animals. She even let me get pink sheets.

I remember I was excited when the big truck delivered my bed, even when the beeping noise it made caused me to cover my ears. I ran to the door as Mom opened it. I was jumping up and down when the men finally finished putting my bed together. But when I saw Dad taking my crib apart that night, I got sad. The big bed may have been a futon that was close to the floor, but it still was scary, even with a guardrail and a night-light.

Mom let me line up my stuffed animals on my bed. I had them lined up in order. Against the wall, closest to my head, was Teddy, my protector bear, so I could grab her; then came Abby, my guardian angel bear, followed by Whiskers, my white cat. The last two on that side were Rabbie, my brown rabbit, and Missy, my black horse. Against the guardrail, I lined up Wolfie, my stuffed wolf; Humphry, my humpback whale; Ralphie, my giraffe; and Penny, my penguin. I always had to have them in the same order. I still did not feel safe, so I refused to sleep in the bed. I got up the second Mom left and went looking for her.

Francesca

It was over two months before Mia actually slept in her bed. I tried everything. I made sure that we kept all of our activities calm and quiet for at least two hours before Mia's bedtime. I read stories on transitions to big beds to Mia. I reminded her that she had her stuffed animal guards. We said prayers together every night. I even tried staying with her until she fell asleep. None of this worked.

It really did not make sense because nothing else had changed in Mia's life. We talked to our friends and found that their kids did not have this much trouble transitioning to a bed.

This time was very frustrating for Ben and me. We wondered if we would ever be able to get Mia to bed easily again. I finally turned to a self-help book that recommended a tough approach. Every time Mia got out of bed, I would gently walk her back to bed. I would not say anything to her, and I would not stay with her. After four weeks of this, she finally stayed in bed, but she still had to have her animals lined up in just the right order. If even one was missing or out of place, she could not sleep.

Mia

Yes, I remember there was just enough room for me to squeeze between them. Dad said he did not even know how I had room to sleep. I also insisted that my mom check on me before she went to bed. Of course, she would have anyway.

Francesca

We now know that kids on the autistic spectrum frequently need order, such as lining up their animals, and they may also need some form of pressure to sleep. Some use a heavy quilt for this; however, in Hawaii, a heavy quilt would be too hot. Mia substituted the stuffed animals and her sheet. Also, having trouble adjusting to changes is a symptom of Asperger's.

Mia was sixteen months old when she surprised me. She had just helped me move some of her stuffed animals so we had room to sit on her bed with our backs against the wall. As part of her bedtime ritual, I asked, "What story shall we read tonight?"

"*Time for Bed*," Mia said. "I read."

"Okay," I said as I put it in her lap. "You read to me."

Mia took the book in her small hands and opened it to the first page. Then she started reading the words, "It's time for bed, little mouse. Little mouse, darkness is falling all over the house … It's time to sleep, little pup, little pup. If you don't sleep soon, the sun will be up! … The stars on high are shining bright. Sweet dreams, my darling, sleep well … good night."

"Wow," I said as I clapped loudly. "That's amazing, Mia. You read the whole book by yourself. Yay!" Ben came into the room to see what all of the excitement was about. "Hey, what's going on in here?"

"Mia just read *Time for Bed* to me. She knows the entire book word for word, and she even turned the pages at the right time," I said.

"Wow! Mia, do you know how incredible you are?" Ben asked as he picked Mia up and danced around the room with her.

"Daddy, what's incredible?" Mia asked.

"You are," Ben said. On seeing Mia's puzzled look, he said, "It means that you're very smart for your age."

Mia was smiling from ear to ear as she said, "I love you, Daddy."

"I love you too. Now isn't it really time for your bed?" Ben asked.

Mia nodded. "Yes, Daddy, after prayers."

After we said prayers and Mia was tucked into bed, I went to help Ben load the dishwasher. He stopped to hug me. "Didn't you just get her that book?"

"Yes, I bought it two days ago. It's amazing that she memorized it after only hearing it twice."

Ben said, "I've heard of kids who are memorizing short picture books at age three, but I don't think I've ever heard of a sixteen-month-old memorizing an entire book, especially after only hearing it twice. We have a very smart girl."

"Yes, I already knew that, but it's nice that you see it too," I said.

We would learn that excellent rote memory and the ability to echo language are two more hallmarks of Asperger's. Some are better with auditory memory while others are more visual. Mia had memorized the book and was able to echo the words she had heard.

Mia and I called Grandma and Grandpa the next day, and she "read" for them too. They both clapped and told her how proud they were of her.

We invited Ah Ma and Ah Gung to come see her "read," and of course they did.

Ah Gung said, "Wow, what a memory you have!" with a little laugh.

Ah Ma clapped and said, "How many other children can memorize like that at your age?"

At eighteen months old, Mia had a large vocabulary. She was speaking in short sentences to us and to Ah Ma, Ah Gung, and her Uncle Kevin. She also knew all of her colors and shapes. She had memorized her colors by noting who in her family had that color as his or her favorite. Pink remained her favorite, and she even remembered that it was Grandma's favorite too.

Mia could also count to ten. She could say the alphabet, and she was beginning to recognize her letters and numbers.

Ben and I decided that Mia needed to interact with other kids. None of our friends had kids. My nieces and my nephew lived far away, and Ben's brothers did not have kids yet, so we signed Mia up for a playgroup, but she would not talk to the other kids.

Mia

They scared me, especially when we met at my house and they touched my toys. Even when we went to the park with the big slide and the monkey bars, they were too rambunctious for me. Their loud voices hurt my ears, and they got too close to me when I was waiting in line for the slide, so I stopped going down the slide to avoid them. I tried to stay as far away from them as possible.

Francesca

Mia and I were part of the playgroup for four months. Because she was two to four months younger than the other children, I thought that was the reason she did not interact with them. Both Ben and our pediatrician said not to worry.

Mia

When our playgroup broke up two months before my second birthday, Mom enrolled me in a mommy's respite group. It met for one and a half hours two days a week at the Baptist church. The teachers were nice, and I enjoyed making crafts with them.

I did not play with the kids. They were loud and rough. About a month after I began going there, one of the little boys bit me twice on my cheek. I did not cry, so the teachers did not even notice until Mom came to get me.

Francesca

When Mia started at the Baptist church, the kids were her age. Yet, Mia did not interact with them. Then one day, when I was picking her up, I saw teeth marks in two different spots on Mia's right cheek. I was horrified. I turned to the teachers. "What happened to Mia? Who bit her?"

The teachers looked at Mia. "Mia, why didn't you tell us someone bit you? Who did this?"

She pointed to the little boy who had bitten her. They went to talk to his mother.

I turned to Mia and said, "Let's get you home, wash your cheek, and apply some ice. I can't believe the teachers weren't watching better. You must have cried. I think I will keep you home on Wednesday."

Mia

Mom didn't ask me if I cried, so I didn't tell her. I didn't tell Mom that it didn't hurt that much either, because I was looking forward to staying home.

Francesca

We now know that children with Asperger's may show little or no response to pain that others would consider unbearable. They may not know how they got a bruise or a cut.

When Ben got home, I told him what had happened. He too suggested keeping Mia home. He said I should call around to see if there was a program somewhere else.

I made phone calls the next day, but everyone had waiting lists for their programs. I put her name on the shortest list, which was at the Congregational church. Well-meaning friends told me that a kid biting other kids was all part of growing up.

When Mia went back to school, the teachers promised to keep a closer eye on her. I told Mia to be sure to tell a teacher if another kid hurt her in any way. I still did not feel good about leaving her.

The next week, the other school called to say that they had a spot for Mia. I took Mia to see the new school. They had swings, which got Mia's vote, so I moved her.

Mia

The Congregational school went from 8:00 AM until 2:30 PM two days a week. I did make friends at the new school, but I never liked to nap there. They tried to make me take a nap after lunch. I hated sleeping on the floor among strangers, so I would refuse to sleep. My teachers got mad at me and kept me in for afternoon recess.

Mom told me to just close my eyes and pretend to sleep so I could have recess with my friends.

Francesca

Even Mia's trouble napping was probably related to her Asperger's. Kids with Asperger's are more sensitive to their environment, so the hard floor and being with other people really did affect Mia.

Chapter V
MY LITTLE BROTHER

My Uncle Kevin wasn't around much for a few months. Auntie Renee was with him every time he was. Mom and Dad told me that they were busy planning their wedding. On my second birthday, Uncle Kevin and Auntie Renee asked me to be their flower girl. The wedding was a month later. After the wedding, they would move to the mainland. Being a flower girl sounded like fun.

Grandma and Grandpa and Auntie Angie and Uncle Dave came for my second birthday party. Uncle Kevin said they were invited to the wedding too if they could make it back.

Grandma said, "We wouldn't miss it for the world."

Auntie Angie said, "I second that."

The week before the wedding, Uncle Lester and Auntie Diane came. They helped me practice by making paper petals for me to toss from a basket as I walked down the hall. It was fun, but it was scary when I actually had to walk down the aisle with people staring at me, so I cried and ran to Mom, who carried me down the aisle while I buried my face in her shoulder.

I wanted the wedding to be over so people would quit trying to talk to me. Grandma seemed to understand because when Mom was dancing with Dad, she just held me in her lap and kissed the top of my head like Mom sometimes did. She didn't say anything, but I knew she loved me no matter what.

I heard Ah Ma talking to Mom. "It's too bad the photographer did not get a picture of Mia coming down the aisle before she ran to you."

I felt like I had failed her somehow.

Everyone returned home a couple of days after the wedding. I missed Grandma the most. She so understood me.

A few weeks later, I realized that I would not get to see Uncle Kevin so much anymore. I cried when I talked to him on the phone. Uncle Kevin said that he was living closer to Uncle Lester and Auntie Diane. He said that now I could see all of them when I came to visit. But even I knew things would not be the same.

Uncle Kevin's move was not the only big change in store for me. My mom's belly was growing. I thought Mom was getting fat.

Francesca

My dad was still doing okay, but after our talk at Angie's wedding, I knew I had to have a second child soon if I wanted Dad to see him or her. Ben and I had discussed the timing for several weeks after we came back from Denver. Finally, we decided that it would be best if Mia was between two and three years old before we had another child.

We were worried about how Mia would handle being a big sister. We had read books that advised waiting to tell her until closer to my due date. She started asking me questions about my belly after Kevin's wedding. I was five months pregnant then.

Mia

Mom and Dad started reading books to me about being a big sister. It sounded like fun until Mom stopped taking me to run with our dog. I missed our runs. Instead, we now walked or just stayed home.

Next, Mom and Dad asked me if I wanted to move to the bigger bedroom down the hall. They had painted stars on the ceiling for me. It was pretty, but I was worried about moving. The room was too far away from Mom and Dad.

Francesca

Both Ben and I assured Mia that we would still have a baby monitor in her room. We promised we would be able to hear her if she needed us. Unfortunately, Mia was still scared because the room was not next to ours.

Mia

I was very scared, but I agreed to move to the new room. For the first three months, I could not sleep. I kept hearing things outside, and I could not hear Mom and Dad because they were too far away. When I did sleep, I would have nightmares and wake up screaming. Sometimes, I would not even remember waking up. Other times, I would be afraid to go to bed the next night because the previous night's dream was still too vivid in my mind.

Francesca

Mia drove me crazy the first three months she was in her new room. I had to get up at least once a night to sit with her when she woke up screaming. I was six months pregnant with her little brother then and very tired. She continued to have nightmares through the rest of my pregnancy.

Mia

One night when I woke up, my mom was so tired that she let me go back to her bed to sleep. I still could not go back to sleep. Dad's snoring was too loud, and Mom's belly was too big to allow me much room.

I do not know if I made my little brother anxious or if I was the anxious one. I could sense that he was ready to be born. All I know is that my mom's labor started that night. Instead of Mom sleeping with her arms around me, she and Dad dropped me off at my grandparents' house to sleep. How could anyone sleep after that?

Francesca

My labor did start when Mia was in bed with me, but I think it was just a coincidence. I was already thirty-seven weeks into the pregnancy. My feet were swollen so badly that I could not wear any of my shoes. I had Velcro slippers (rubber sandals) that I had let all the way out. I was ready to have Caleb (Mia's baby brother). I wanted my body back.

Mia

The next day, I waited anxiously for word of my mother and my new baby brother. Ah Ma finally got the call at 1:00 PM that I had a baby brother who was anxious to meet me. I just wanted to see my mom to make sure she was okay. Ah Ma was more concerned with my baby brother.

When we got to the hospital, my little brother was in the nursery with Dad. Mom was not there. My dad held up my baby brother for me to see. I just wanted someone to tell me where my mother was.

Finally, Ah Ma took me to see Mom. Mom was very pale. I was worried about her.

Francesca

I was pale when Caleb was born, as I had lost a lot of blood. I told Mia that I did not get much sleep during the night, but that I would be okay. I did not know how pale I really looked until I saw Caleb's first baby pictures later.

When they moved me to another room, I let Mia ride in the wheelchair with me. As we approached the nursery, I felt Mia's body tense up and saw her frown and turn away. I suspected Mia was experiencing jealousy of her new baby brother. "What's wrong?"

"Mommy, I don't want to stop. I already saw him. Ah Ma made me stop here before I came to see you."

I assured Mia, "I want to spend a few minutes with you. We don't need to stop at the nursery because they will bring him to my room soon."

Unfortunately, they did not bring him for a while. I needed to have pain medication before he was born, and he was a very sleepy baby. They had to watch him for two hours to make sure that his breathing was okay.

While we waited, I looked at Mia and patted my bed for her to sit by me. As she climbed up, I asked, "Did you get any sleep last night?"

"I slept some. I was too worried about you to sleep well."

I put my arms around Mia and hugged her tight as I kissed the top of her head. "Mia, I love you very much. I promise I am okay."

After waiting in my room for thirty minutes, my mother-in-law looked at my father-in-law and said, "We need to leave soon so we can all get some sleep." Then she turned to Mia, "Tell your mother good-bye. You really shouldn't be on her bed anyway. Your mommy needs her rest."

"Mom," I said, "Mia really needs to wait for Caleb to come from the nursery."

I gave Ben a sideways knowing glance because my mother-in-law was not likely to listen to me.

He agreed. "Yes, Mom, she needs to see her brother."

My in-laws reluctantly waited with Mia so she could meet her brother.

Mia

Ah Ma kept trying to get me to move away from my mother's bed.

Mom said, "Mia is fine just where she is."

As she continued to hug me, I looked up at Mom. "When are you coming home?"

She kissed the top of my head again before she explained, "Your baby brother and I will need to spend one night in the hospital. Daddy will be home with you tonight so you will be able to sleep in your own bed."

Dad said, "I will be taking a week off from work. I will be able to take you to school and pick you up this week. Mommy and Caleb will be home tomorrow. Remember we talked to you about what would happen when your brother was born."

I loved Dad at that time, but I was always Mommy's girl. I was not happy that she would be away from home.

She saw my sad, worried face and said, "Mia, it will be okay. It's only one night. I will be home soon. You can help me with Caleb when we get home."

Finally, they brought my brother to Mom's room. He had a cap on his head and was wrapped tightly in a blanket. Still, I could see that he looked funny.

I said, "Cal … eb looks funny, and his name is too hard to say. Why does he have fuzz on his body and such red round cheeks? Where is his neck?"

Mom kissed the top of my head and then said, "Mia, we are going to call him Cal. It's easy to say. He was born three weeks early. That's why he has fine body hair. He has a neck, but his neck is too weak to hold up his head yet. When you were born, your neck was too weak to hold up your head too. It's normal. Eventually, his neck will get stronger." She showed me how to support my little brother's neck so that he would not hurt his neck or head. She let me hold Cal in my lap. Dad took a picture of me holding him. Mom thought it was so sweet.

It was nice to hold my brother, but he was heavy. When I said so, Ah Ma took Cal. I think she thought I would drop him. Mom just smiled at me and reminded me that I had a present to give to my brother.

I had picked out a blue bear for Cal before he was born. Mom had remembered to bring it to the hospital for me to give to him. With a little help from Dad and Mom, Cal had a present for me too.

Cal gave me a doll that I had been wanting. I kissed him. Mom leaned over and kissed me as I was now standing by her bed.

Then Ah Ma said it was time to leave. Mom saw my puzzled look as I asked, "Why can't I stay with Mommy? I don't want to go! I want to stay here."

Dad said, "You have school tomorrow so you need to go with Ah Ma and Ah Gung so you can eat dinner and bathe. I'll come get you before bedtime."

"No school!" I stomped my foot. "Jessica got to stay home when her sister was born."

Francesca
I knew Ben would not know how to handle this, so I held out my arms, and Mia stepped into them. "You look very tired. I know you didn't get much sleep last night. You need to get a good night's sleep so you can help me when I come home tomorrow. I think I can talk Daddy into letting you stay home tomorrow if you go with Ah Ma and Ah Gung now, right, Dad?"

Ben followed my lead and nodded, as even he knew to choose his battles, especially when he was outnumbered.

Out of the corner of my eye, I saw my mother-in-law's disapproving look.

I didn't care. I knew Mia hadn't slept the night before; and because she was unhappy, sending her to their house without offering her something to look forward to did not seem like a good idea.

Mia

I kissed Mom, Dad, and my little brother good-bye. I really was sad to leave them. It seemed as if my brother was stealing my parents.

The next day, my mom came home as promised, but she was not her usual happy self. She was still very pale.

Also, I had woken up with a bad cold. Normally, my mom would have been concerned about me. Now, it seemed like she was more concerned about my not giving my cold to my brother.

She put a plastic bag, a box of tissues, and baby wipes by her so that I could blow my nose, wipe my hands, and throw my tissue and baby wipe in the bag to avoid giving my germs to my brother. She had never cared about my germs before. And before this, she always held me when I was sick. Now it seemed like she was always too busy nursing my brother to hold me.

My brother ate every hour and a half so Mom had little time for me, even when I wasn't sick. She did not even pick me up from school anymore. My dad dropped me off at school, and my grandparents picked me up.

*　　*　　*

"Mia, I know you felt abandoned when Cal was first born. I wanted to be there for you, and I really tried to spend as much time with you as I could, but I was so weak. I had lost so much blood that I was taking high doses of iron every day. I was even more tired than I had been before Cal was born.

"I tried to explain to you that I was at greater risk for illnesses and that Cal was also at risk since he was so young. If he had gotten sick, his doctor would have admitted him to the hospital for testing. I would have had to go stay with him. Then I would have had more time away from you. But I knew at the time that you were too young to understand."

*　　*　　*

Mia

Mom did try to explain things to me at the time, but all I really understood was that my brother was more important than I was. Ah Ma and Ah Gung spent time with me, but they were a poor substitute as they did not understand that I needed downtime. I missed my mom's calm understanding when she picked me up from school. I also missed things we did together before Cal was born like lying on a beach mat in the backyard to watch clouds to see what pictures God was painting.

Besides, Ah Ma and Ah Gung seemed distracted. Mom and Dad finally told me that Ah Ma and Ah Gung were distracted because Uncle Lester and Auntie Diane were going to have a baby any day. They wanted to go to visit them so they could be there when my little cousin was born. Mom said that Auntie Renee had also recently told them that she was pregnant, so Uncle Kevin would soon be a dad as well.

Eventually, my brother was six weeks old, and my mom was able to pick me up from school again. I was glad, but it still was not like before, as now she always had my brother with her. Mom had no choice but to bring Cal when she picked me up because my grandparents were visiting my uncles and aunties and my new cousin, Karl, in California.

Now I was jealous of Karl as well as Cal. After all, Karl had my Ah Ma and Ah Gung, and he did not have a sibling. He was so lucky. He did not have to share his parents with someone else.

After Mom picked me up from school, we always went straight home so Mom could feed Cal. Once Cal ate, he took a one-and-a-half-hour to two-hour nap.

This was my time to have Mom to myself. We would pretend that we were going on an airplane trip, and the couch became our airline seats. Sometimes we had tea parties together and even had real food. Mom even put the beach mats down in the backyard so we could cloud watch a couple of times.

It was fun to play with Mom again. I just wished that our time alone together were longer. On the days that I did not go to school, it felt like she could not wait for me to take my nap so she could have time without me around.

*   *   *

"Mia, I am sorry that you felt that way. I loved every second of our time together. I was just too tired to be as enthusiastic as I would have liked to be. I was still anemic at the time from all of the blood loss. At times, I felt as if I would never regain my energy. Cal continued to nurse every one and a half hours even during the night until he was four months old. I unfortunately continued to have very low iron levels that made me even more tired. I took iron for a total of three months before I finally felt better. I had also received bad news when Cal was two months old. Your grandpa's cancer had returned, and he was not doing well."

*   *   *

Mia

Other kids in my class had mothers who went on excursions with us. My mom could never go because she had no one to watch my brother. My grandparents came back from their trip, but since Mom was nursing Cal, they could not watch him for more than an hour. He would not take a bottle. No siblings could come on excursions. Little did I know that life was about to change even more.

Chapter VI
THE UNTHINKABLE

Francesca

We were planning to visit the mainland for Easter, so my parents could meet Cal. A week before we were to leave, the unthinkable happened.

As Dad had predicted, he did not live to see my second child. We all had to pack quickly to go to his funeral because the only flight we could get out of Honolulu left late that night. Neither Mia nor I slept on the plane. I was too busy crying so I told Ben to nap so at least one of us would be awake enough to drive when we got there.

Mia

The flight was awful because Mom was crying quietly most of the way. There was too much noise from the flight attendants moving up and down the aisles to assist people, and there was no room to stretch out. I couldn't sleep. Mom told me that she never was able to sleep well on planes either, although she said she did usually take short naps.

Luckily, Dad and Cal slept. When we arrived, we took the shuttle to get the rental car Mom had reserved before we left home. We had a van that already had a booster seat for me and a car seat for Cal. Mom put Cal in his car seat while I got in my booster seat and Dad loaded the luggage in the back.

Then Dad drove us toward Grandma's house. Along the way, Mom suggested that we check into a hotel so she and I could nap. She knew that there would be too many people at Grandma's for us to do that. So we stopped at a hotel and napped for two hours before driving the rest of the way to Grandma's house.

When we got to Grandma's house, there were tons of people. All of my aunts and uncles were there. I really did not know any of the people except for Grandma and Auntie Angie and Uncle Dave. I knew them because they had come to Hawaii twice. I also still talked to Grandma on the phone all the time, and she sent me pictures. Mom talked to my aunties and uncles every week, but I rarely talked to them because I didn't like talking on the phone. It was a sensory thing for me, but they just assumed it was shyness because I hadn't seen them in so long.

I hadn't seen my cousins or some of my aunts and uncles since I was six months old. Mom had been unable to travel because she was pregnant with Cal and afterward Cal nursed so often. I think she was also afraid to travel with two kids without Dad. Since Dad had taken time off when Cal was born, he could not just take off again so soon. He had decided that he could take enough time off for our planned trip over Easter.

Grandma seemed much older than she had at Uncle Kevin's wedding. She did not seem to know what she was supposed to be doing. She kept asking Mom and Auntie Brenda for advice.

Mom was hugging everyone, and everyone was crying. I was grumpy and just wanted to get away. Dad said that we had to stay for a while.

I noticed that Cal and I were the only kids. I asked Auntie Angie where all my cousins were. She said that they were in school but that they would be there that night, as they would go to the viewing.

I asked what a viewing was. She explained that it was a time for people to express their sadness that Grandpa was dead, and she said his body would be on display. I did not like the sound of that.

Mom and Dad said that I did not have to go to the viewing, but I would have to go to the funeral the next day. Mom had to go to the viewing, though, so Dad agreed he would stay with Cal and me.

We then went back to the hotel so Mom could get a couple more hours of sleep. Then, that afternoon, we all got dressed up and went back to Grandma's house for dinner. There was a lot of food. I was a fussy eater; but luckily, they had fried chicken and mashed potatoes, which I loved, so I ate.

Francesca
Mia didn't like foods that were mixed together like casseroles, but she ate one-topping pizzas. She also would eat macaroni and cheese and spaghetti; otherwise, she did not eat anything with sauce. She didn't like foods with strong odors either. Mia's picky eating was also a sign of Asperger's syndrome. For Mia, it was related to her sensory issues.

Mia
My cousins were at Grandma's too. Melanie, the one with whom I had played when I was a baby, wanted to know why I wasn't going to the viewing. I told

her that Mom had said that I did not have to go. She said Uncle Paul and Auntie Ann were making her go. My cousin Jenny said that Auntie Brenda and Uncle Brad made her go to her first viewing and funeral last year when her other grandpa died and she had been my age. She said that I was lucky that I didn't have to go to the viewing.

After I talked to Jenny, I went looking for Mom. I found her coming out of the bathroom. "Thank you for allowing me to skip the viewing. Jenny told me that she had to go to a viewing last year. Melanie said Uncle Paul and Auntie Ann are making her go tonight."

"Mia, I went to a viewing when I was young, and I had nightmares for a week afterward. I didn't want to do that to you. I would love to have your father there, but I want to protect you. Besides, your daddy had a traumatic experience as a child too. When Ah Gung's dad died, they made your father stand beside the open coffin for hours while everyone filed past. We understand that the viewing is not the best place for you and Cal to be. Now I need to find your daddy and brother."

Francesca

I fed Cal and then pumped milk for Ben to feed Cal again before he went to bed. Luckily, he had finally started taking an occasional bottle, although he still did not like it. I then went to help Mom get ready for Dad's viewing. She was having trouble deciding what to wear.

George drove us to the viewing. I had never liked looking at bodies at funerals. I certainly did not want to see my dad now. I wanted to remember him as he was before he became ill, not as he looked in the coffin.

Unfortunately, as his child, I had no choice but to be in the room with his body when people came by to pay their respects. The whole time, I kept thinking about my last conversation with Dad. He was so happy that he would get to see Cal face-to-face. Now he never would.

Mia

Dad took us back to the hotel, as Uncle George had agreed to drop Mom off at the hotel after the viewing. I could not sleep. I kept seeing this image of my mom standing next to a dead body with people all around her. My dad tried to be understanding, but he was sleepy and did not know what I was thinking. We got grumpy with each other, and neither of us could go to sleep. We ended up watching TV, but there was nothing on for kids, so Dad had to turn it off.

Francesca

When I got back to the hotel, Ben was snoring, Cal was sleeping in his crib, and Mia was wide awake. She hugged me and told me that she loved me and was glad that I was back.

I told Mia to try to go to sleep because I had to pump milk before I could go to bed. I went into the bathroom to try to avoid waking Ben and Cal. I could not stop crying. I took a quick shower hoping that the tears would be gone when I was done and that Mia would be asleep. I was the only one of my siblings at the viewing without my family. I knew Cal was too young for the viewing to affect him, and it seemed that Mia was affected even without going.

To make matters worse, Ben was oblivious to Mia, or else he just did not know how to help. Either way, he shouldn't have gone to sleep until Mia was asleep, but then I remembered that Mia was a light sleeper, so perhaps she was asleep when Ben went to bed.

Mia

I could tell my mom had been crying when she came out of the bathroom. I asked her if seeing a dead body had made her cry.

Francesca

I kissed Mia and put my finger to my lips to remind her that we had to be quiet, as Ben and Cal were asleep. I had her follow me to the bathroom, and I closed the door. Then I tried to explain why I had been crying. I told her that I had always been Grandpa's little girl and that anytime I needed to talk to someone about something, Grandpa was the first person who popped into my mind.

Mia

I did not understand this. I kept trying to get an image of someone popping out of my head. Did this mean they exploded like a firecracker? I did not think so. I asked Mom, and she smiled for the first time that day.

Francesca

Mia did make me smile. "It's an expression, Mia." I hugged her and told her it was time to go to bed, and I walked her back to bed. I sat with her until she finally fell into an exhausted sleep. Then I finally went to bed too.

Cal woke me up during the night, but he went right back to sleep after I fed him. I looked at my sleeping family and thought about how Dad must have felt about us. I said, "I miss you, Dad," and softly cried myself back to sleep.

Mia

The next morning, we all woke up early, ate breakfast, and got dressed in dark clothes. I asked Mom why we had to wear dark clothes. Mom said that in the South, everyone wears dark clothes to funerals. Mom was making me wear an itchy-feeling top and a black skirt. She said that I could not wear blue jeans and a sweatshirt to Grandpa's funeral.

Mom usually removed all of the tags and washed all my clothes twice before I wore them. She knew that I didn't like clothes with elastic or with scratchy seams or material so she was usually good about this too. This time, Mom did not give me a choice, because she did not have an alternate outfit for me to wear. There had not been enough time to do laundry before we left home and my outfit was new.

I was very uncomfortable, but not half as uncomfortable as I was about to be. When we got to the church, there were tons of cars and many people dressed in black. They all came up to my mom and hugged her and told her how sorry they were. Several of them tried to hug me too, but I hid behind my mom.

Soft hugs made my skin crawl. Mom hugged with just the right amount of pressure, not too hard and not too soft. The only other person who hugged the right way was Grandma, although I did tolerate hugs from Dad and from most of Mom's family. Dad wasn't really a hugger either, so I didn't really worry that he didn't hug correctly. Besides, since I was almost three, he rarely hugged me anymore. Somehow, I was too old to hug. I didn't know why, but I really didn't miss his hugs, so it was okay—although I was sure that if Mom stopped hugging, I would miss hers.

Francesca

When we got to the funeral, I told Mia that I had to go into the room where my dad's body was to greet people and that the coffin would be open. I explained, "I don't think that you or Cal should come into the room while the coffin is open. Once the coffin is closed, you will have to come into the room with Daddy and Cal."

I thought, *This is so freaky. Mommy is in the room with Grandpa's open coffin. I am glad that I get to wait with Daddy and Cal.*

The coffin was closed when we went in to join Mom. It was still freaky to be in the room with my grandpa's body. Unfortunately, Mom did not give us an option. We had to be with Grandma and the rest of the family.

We followed the coffin into the church, and then we sat on the front pew while the minister talked about Grandpa for over an hour and then said some prayers and someone sang some songs. My mom cried softly and kept blotting her eyes with a tissue.

The next thing I knew, we were following Grandpa's coffin out the door. I was relieved because I thought that meant that the funeral was over. Boy was I wrong!

When we got outside, there was a line of men making an arch. We had to walk through the arch. Then we had to get in our car, which was directly behind a long black car. I saw my Grandpa's coffin slide into the long black car. Dad helped Grandma into our car.

I asked my mom, "How did our car get behind the long black car? What is with the men, and where are they taking Grandpa's coffin?"

Mom was too busy crying to answer.

Dad said, "The men are Shriners. Grandpa was very active with the Shriner's temple and the Masonic lodge. The men are members of Grandpa's temple and lodge. They are here to show their respect for Grandpa."

Mom blew her nose and blotted her tears. "These organizations help kids. Grandpa loved helping kids. We are following Grandpa's coffin to the cemetery."

On the way to the cemetery, Dad explained, "Once we reach the cemetery, we will walk behind Grandpa's coffin until it is placed on the grave site. Then, we will sit down in front of the coffin while the minister gives another short sermon and says another prayer."

I asked, "What is a grave site? Why is there another sermon and prayer?"

Francesca

Mia had so many questions that I had to dry my tears again so I could explain things to her. I said, "The grave site is the place that they will bury Grandpa. As Dad said, there will be an additional sermon and prayer. This probably started in the old days when people thought that you had to be buried in sacred ground."

"Mommy, what is sacred ground?"

"Mia, sacred ground is land that is considered to be holy or blessed. After the service, the coffin will be lowered into the ground. Sometimes the family files by the coffin one more time to say good-bye. As it is being lowered into the ground, the family might choose to add a handful of dirt or a rose to the coffin."

Mia

As you may have guessed, I was now totally freaked out! I wished I were Cal. He was sound asleep in his infant seat. Dad was carrying him.

I had always had an excessively vivid imagination. I was picturing my grandpa as he looked in pictures at home. Only now, I saw a lid over him and dirt being shoveled on top of him. For a girl who was two months away from her third birthday, this was a very scary image.

I somehow survived the graveside service. I think I must have blocked it all out. I honestly do not remember any of it.

The next thing I knew, we were back in the car on the way to Grandma's house with Cal crying because he had just woken up. He was either hungry or needed a diaper change or both. I never knew what his cries meant. I only knew that I hated him at this moment. He was spared the entire funeral.

When we arrived at Grandma's house, there were still too many people and lots of food. Grandpa's friends came to Grandma's house after the funeral. They told Mom stories about Grandpa. People remembered how kind he was. Many people told funny stories about him. Some even made Mom laugh.

It was good to see Mom laugh. She had cried so much since we got the phone call that Grandpa had died. I had begun to wonder if she would ever laugh again. I cherished every moment of laughter in the weeks ahead, as Mom shed many tears over Grandpa's death.

Francesca
The day of the funeral, we moved from the hotel to Mom's house. We stayed to help her for a couple weeks. Angie and Dave stayed too.

We spent Easter with Mom as we had originally planned. Mom and Angie helped Mia dye Easter eggs on Saturday before Easter, and the whole family was there Easter Sunday. We all went to church together and stopped by the cemetery to put an Easter lily on Dad's grave.

Mia
Grandma made me feel special and loved. She really tried to make sure that I had a fun Easter by dying eggs with Auntie Angie and me. She even had paints for me to paint the eggs, and she let me make a big mess doing it. She laughed about how I looked with paint on my face. I loved her so much for doing this when I knew she was sad because I heard her crying in the bathroom and I saw her wipe an occasional tear when she thought I wasn't looking.

After church on Easter, all of my aunts and uncles and cousins came to Grandma's for lunch. Afterward, Grandma and Auntie Angie hid eggs for my cousins and me to have an Easter egg hunt.

That night after my cousins left, Grandma gave me a wrapped present and told me that she and Grandpa had bought it for me months before and she hoped it would remind me of how much he loved me. When I ripped it open, I found a very soft pink bunny. I named her Rosie. I hugged her tight, and Grandma smiled as she wiped away a tear. Then she hugged me and told me how glad she was that I was there, as she loved me very much.

The closer it got to time to return home, the sadder Grandma seemed. She said that she was worrying about being alone. Grandma had never lived alone before. This had Mom concerned. I overheard her talking to my Auntie Angie about it. They both talked to Auntie Brenda, Uncle George, and Uncle Paul. Mom told me not to worry because they had a plan.

Francesca
George agreed to let Mom stay with his family for a few days when we left. Then, Brenda would let Mom stay with her for a couple of weeks. If Mom still did not want to return home, Paul would take her to stay with him for a week or she would come out to visit us. We did not want Angie to have to be involved yet, as she was now five months pregnant with her first child. Our plan made me feel a little better. However, I was still concerned about how Mom would manage when she finally returned home.

On the day we left, we drove Mom to George's house and said our good-byes. Angie and Dave had left the night before. Mom seemed okay, but I knew that she really was not. I hugged and kissed her and promised to call her. I really hated to leave her, but Mia had to return to school and Ben had to get back to his patients.

Chapter VII
A Time of Adjustments

Mia

Once we got back home, I had to return to preschool. It was hard to go back. I was grumpy for the first week.

* * *

"Mia, that was because we had been on East Coast time and our bodies had to adjust to being back on Hawaii time. Being back in school helped you to get back on schedule. It also helped me, as I had to get up with you on the mornings that you had school."

* * *

Mia

I hated getting up on the days I had school. Mom let me sleep a little later on the days I didn't. One morning, I woke up because I heard Mom crying from all the way down the hall. I crawled out of my bed, opened my door, and snuck down the hall to her room. I opened the door to see Mom sitting on the bed with her head bent and her hands covering her face. I climbed onto the bed and put my arm around her. "Mommy, why are you crying?"

Francesca

As I felt Mia's little arm around my back, I looked up. "Mia, I miss Grandpa. I hate it that Grandpa never got to see Cal or Auntie Angie's baby. When Auntie Angie got married, he told me that he would not live to see my second child. He was right."

I hugged Mia back as I dabbed at my eyes with a tissue. She looked up at me. "We didn't see Grandpa that much. Didn't you send him pictures of Cal?"

I reached over, pulled her into my lap, and kissed the top of her head. "Mia, my entire life my dad had only been a phone call away. I never went more than a week without talking to him. If I did not call him, then he always called me. I miss hearing his voice. While it is good that Grandpa got to see pictures of Cal, seeing pictures of someone is not the same as seeing them in person."

She looked up and said, "I know what will cheer you up. Let's call Grandma. She saw Cal. You can hear her voice."

I gently eased Mia off my lap as I got up to get another tissue. I blew my nose and threw it away. "Yes, I'm grateful for that. I love my mom, but I was always Dad's girl. Anytime I was unsure of anything, I always called my dad. He always listened and gave good advice. Then he let me make my own decisions."

Mia

I followed Mom as she walked to the bathroom to wash her face and hands. I still did not understand. "Mommy, you're a grown-up. Why do you need someone else's advice?"

"Everyone needs someone to bounce ideas off of sometimes," she said as she finished drying her face and hands. "Let's go call Grandma."

We did call Grandma, and that seemed to cheer Mom up, but I kept trying to picture ideas bouncing off Grandpa. I could not picture this, and the thought of Grandpa reminded me that he was in the ground. That scared me.

Just the thought of this would keep me awake at night. When I did fall asleep, I would have nightmares of my mom bouncing on my grandfather's grave. I would wake up terrified and run to Mom's bed to wake her up. She would ask what was wrong. I could never tell her because I did not want to see her cry. Sometimes I had two nightmares a night.

Francesca

I got grumpy because I was still getting up with Cal and now Mia too! I tried to comfort Mia when she had nightmares. Yet, when she got up the second time in the same night, I would get frustrated with her. I was especially frustrated when this happened several nights in a row, as it sometimes did.

Mia

Dad was getting frustrated with me too, as he would wake up sometimes when Mom did, and he had to go to work the next day. Sometimes, he would yell at me to go back to bed. Mom was usually more willing to walk me back to bed, but after several nights of this, even she would tell me to stay in bed. Occasionally, she would let me stay in her bed for a while. But I eventually had to go back to my bed, as Mom would have to nurse Cal. At least Mom would walk me back to my bed and tuck me in.

I was starting to resent Cal because his crib was still in Mom and Dad's room while my room was all the way down the hall. Mom reminded me that she could hear me on the baby monitor, but I still wished I could sleep with them. Mom said that there was not room and that whenever Cal woke up to nurse, he would wake me up.

Francesca

I felt sorry for Mia, and I felt really bad when I got grumpy. Then I remembered the trouble we had with getting her to transition from her crib. The expert's advice worked then, so I knew I had to stick with it again. I stopped speaking to Mia when she got up. Instead, I gently walked her back to bed. It still took several weeks before she slept through the night again.

Mia

I was still afraid to go to sleep at night. Mom spent extra time with me at bedtime, since I wasn't getting up during the night. I didn't tell her that I still had nightmares sometimes. Now I hugged Rosie, my pink bunny, tightly and prayed for protection since I knew Mom would not let me be with her.

I was sleepy at school, so I actually napped. I finally got used to my school. I enjoyed playing with my friends at recess.

One day, Mom announced that she was taking me to look at a new school. She said that my school did not have a prekindergarten class. Mom explained that I would need this class before I applied to Dad's school. She said I would learn to read at the new school.

I knew that Ah Ma, Ah Gung, and Dad were the ones who wanted me to go to Dad's school. They always acted like only two schools existed on the island. Of course, that wasn't really true. They meant that as far as they were concerned, only two were any good. Ah Gung had been telling Mom since before I was born how important my education was. I did not want to leave my friends, but I still wanted Ah Ma, Ah Gung, and Dad to love me. I wasn't sure they would if I didn't go to the right school. I knew Mom would love me no matter what.

Francesca

I was concerned because I knew the new school was more academic, but I also knew that Ben's school would not accept her if she did not do well on their test the next year. Since it was so important to Ben and his parents and because I knew how smart Mia was, I relented.

I tried to prepare Mia for the move. I took her to meet her new teacher. She seemed nice, and there were plenty of interesting toys in her classroom.

Mia

I was hopeful that I would like the new school. Then I heard that I had to go to school every day instead of just two days a week. I panicked. I asked Mom when I would have time to play with her and to help her with Cal. She said that the new school only went until just after lunch so I would have time after school. She said that she and Dad had decided that it was the best school for me. So I said good-bye to my old school friends and prepared for my first day at the new school.

I was in for three surprises as my first day at All Saints Preschool and Kindergarten approached. First, Mom informed me that Dad would drop me off on his way in to work. Next, she said that the teacher I had met would not be teaching for the summer, so I would have a different teacher when I started. Third, I learned that I would have to eat the school lunch instead of taking home lunch.

I was not happy about any of these things. Except for the first six weeks after Cal was born, Mom had always taken me to school. I had been able to sleep until 7:00 AM, as my old school did not start until 8:00 AM. The new school started at 7:30 AM. My old school required you to bring home lunch so I always had food I liked.

When the first day of school finally arrived, I was grumpy. I had been unable to go to sleep until late the night before because of all of my fears. Also, I was not a morning person. When I arrived at school, I found out that my new teacher had a mean face and a mean voice. Her name was Ms. Mein.

For the first hour of school, Ms. Mein read to us and then made us circle picture answers about what she had read. Then she let us have thirty minutes of free time inside playing at either the dress-up area, the Play-Doh area, the puzzle area, or the construction area, which had building blocks and toy trucks. The classroom was too loud during free time even when Ms. Mein reminded us to use our inside voices. We spent the next hour drawing and coloring, which was quieter at least. Then we had an hour on the playground.

After three and a half hours, it was lunchtime. I was horrified to learn that lunch was a hamburger. Hamburger was a food that I had never eaten, so I refused to eat. Ms. Mein said that I had to at least taste the food. I still refused, so she moved me to a table in a corner by myself. She put the tray in front of me and told me that I had to stay there until I tasted my food. I sat there for the full thirty minutes of lunchtime without touching my food.

Ms. Mein came to my table three times. Then, I heard her telling the other kids that it was time to clean up and get ready to go home. I got up. Ms. Mein rushed over to me and told me to sit back down. I said, "But I have to go home too." She said I had to sit there until I ate. I pushed the tray away. She pushed it back toward me. I pushed it away again, but this time, it fell on the floor. Ms. Mein insisted that I help clean it up. I refused, so she made me stay in time-out with the food on the floor while the other kids sat in a circle and sang a good-bye song. I was still sitting there when Mom arrived.

Francesca

When I went to pick up Mia, I did not see her at first. I asked a little girl if she knew where Mia was. She pointed to a table in a dark corner. Mia was sitting with her back to me, so I walked over to tap her on the shoulder. She looked up. She had her arms crossed, and she looked angry. Then she realized it was me and jumped up to hug me.

Just then, Ms. Mein rushed up to me. "Are you her mother?"

"Yes, I am. I'm here to take her home. Mia, go get your shoes on so we can go."

"Ms. Lung, Mia cannot go home yet. I need to talk to you. Would you please follow me? Mia, you stay there."

I followed Ms. Mein as she walked quickly toward the office. When she got there, she held the door open for me to enter. Once the door closed, she looked at me like I must be the worst mother alive. "Ms. Lung, Mia threw her lunch tray at me when I tried to get her to eat today. She cannot go home until she cleans up the mess and apologizes."

I went back to talk to Mia. I squatted down to her level and asked, "Mia, why did you throw your lunch tray at Ms. Mein? That is not like you. Please explain."

Mia

I thought once Mom came, we could just leave, but I was wrong. I crossed my arms again and looked down as I said, "Mommy, I did not throw the tray."

Francesca

I wanted to believe Mia because she had never lied to me, but I had read that this was the age when children made up stories to get out of trouble. I gently grabbed Mia under the chin and forced her to face me. With raised eyebrows, I said, "Mia, you have always been good about telling the truth, so tell me how it got on the floor."

"I pushed the tray, and it fell," she said as I let her chin go.

"Why did you push it? You know better."

Mia's voice rose as she said, "She tried to make me eat hamburger. I did not want to die!"

I was puzzled. "I know you've never eaten hamburger, but what is this about not wanting to die?"

"The kids in Seattle died when they ate hamburgers."

"Mia, you were only a baby when that happened. How do you even remember it?"

"I just do."

"Beef is checked better now, and this hamburger is well cooked. You would not die from eating it. Let's explain things to Ms. Mein and go home."

Mia hid behind me as I walked up to Ms. Mein who looked at her and asked, "Mia, did you clean up the mess?"

I said, "Ms. Mein, Mia is sorry, but she had a good reason for not eating hamburger today. She thought if she ate it, she would die like those children in Seattle a couple of years ago."

Ms. Mein looked at me like I had lost my mind. "What? Do you let her get away with this behavior at home?"

I said, "Ms. Mein, Mia never acts like this. She just did not understand that hamburger is safe to eat. She was just trying to get the tray away from her, not push it on the floor or on you."

Ms. Mein looked at me like I must be insane. "Ms. Lung, whatever reasons Mia gave you, she still has to clean up the mess and apologize. Under no circumstances is a child allowed to throw food in my class."

I turned to Mia, and as I took her hand, I said, "Let's go clean up the mess." As we walked away, I added, "Afterward, you'll need to apologize so we can go home."

Mia

So Mom and I cleaned up the mess. Then with Mom holding my hand, I approached Ms. Mein and said, "I am sorry for pushing the tray."

She said, "Mia, I hope you learned something today. I'll see you tomorrow."

On the drive home, I said, "Mommy, I hate that Ms. Mein, and I never want to go back there. She is really mean. She never smiles, and she hates me." I thought Mom would agree, but she didn't.

"Mia, you should not have pushed the tray. At least tomorrow you will not have hamburger for lunch. Ms. Mein hasn't had a chance to get to know you. Give her a chance. You only have her six weeks."

I continued to hate Ms. Mein. She still tried to force me to eat sometimes.

Mom convinced her to leave me alone if I at least tried a bite of my food. I really hated lunchtime. It was torture. Just so you know, I was not being a brat. The truth was that I had to have my food at just the right temperature to eat it, and some foods were just the wrong color, the wrong texture, or just looked or smelled funny. Even Mom could not understand this, so she did not try to explain it. Mom had several more talks with Ms. Mein during the summer. I know she thought I was a brat, but at least she never put me in an extended time-out again.

Francesca

Finally, the summer was over. Ms. Nicely, the original teacher, was back. She was much more tolerant of Mia's fussy eating habits. She even told me that she did not agree with the school policy of having to try every food. Mia and I both liked her. Plus, one of Mia's old friends started in the fall, so Mia seemed to be adjusting much better.

Mia

I did like school better. I was playing with some of the kids. I liked story time, drawing, playing at the water station, and singing.

Cal was growing up too. He had started to crawl that summer, and now he was trying to walk. He was getting into my toys. I did not like this. Mom said I had to keep my things in my room. I had to make sure no small toys were left on the floor.

Francesca

I tried to help Mia keep her toys off the floor. I even made a game out of it. I set the timer to see who could put away the most toys before the beeper buzzed.

* * *

"Mia, it seemed like you liked the game, especially since I let you beat me most of the time."

"Mom, you let me win? I thought I was faster than you! I liked the game, but I did not like the reason for it. Cal was ruining my life."

"Mia, I can see why it felt that way. Cal wasn't old enough to be a playmate yet, and he was getting into your things."

* * *

Francesca

The first week in December, I told Mia that my mom would be coming for a visit for the holidays. She would arrive in time to see Mia's school Christmas concert.

Mia

I was excited to think Grandma was coming so far just for me. Mom said that Grandma had hurt her ankle two weeks earlier. She warned me that she would need a wheelchair at the airport. She would use a walker afterward. Her younger sister, Great-Aunt Flora, would come with her. Auntie Angie, Uncle Dave, and baby Alex were coming too. They would arrive one day after Grandma.

A week later, we were waiting at the airport for Grandma and Great-Aunt Flora to arrive. They were the last to leave the plane because they had to wait for the flight attendant to get the wheelchair for Grandma.

Francesca

I was shocked to see how much my mom had aged. I knew Dad's death had been hard on her, but I did not realize how hard until I saw her. She had aged at least five years in the past eight months.

When Mom got off the plane, Mia hid behind me and Cal started to cry. I had warned Mom that Mia and Cal might be shy at first since they hadn't seen her in a while. I had also warned the kids that Mom would be in a wheelchair, but I had not thought to warn them that she might look different.

Mia

Grandma looked old and scary. Her face was full of cracks. Great-Aunt Flora had fewer cracks, but I had seen her less than I had seen Grandma.

"Mia, you've grown so much that I would not have known you," Grandma said as she reached into her huge black purse to pull out a small stuffed brown bear. "You are such a pretty little girl. I brought something for you," she said as she held up the bear. "Come here and give me a hug."

When Grandma spoke and then brought out the bear, I knew she was still my grandma, but I was a little scared of the wheelchair.

Mom said, "Mom, I think she is a little scared of the wheelchair, and she hasn't seen you in almost a year. Just give her a little time to get used to you again. Let's go get your luggage and go home. Aunt Flora, I can push the wheelchair. Cal can sit in Mom's lap if that's okay, and Mia can help me push."

"Of course he can," Grandma said as she gently placed the bear back in her bag.

Cal had stopped crying. He touched his grandma's face and said, "GrrrMa," when Mom placed him in her lap.

Grandma smiled and said, "Thanks, Cal. This is the best present." Then she pulled a toy car out of her bag for Cal, which he took with a wide grin.

"Tnk you, GrrrMa," Cal said as he took the car. "Vroooom!"

Mommy said, "Thanks, Mom. He loves cars."

Mommy turned her head toward Aunt Flora and asked, "How was the trip? Did either of you sleep on the plane?"

"I slept," Aunt Flora said. "I think your mom did too, but it was a long flight. It'll be good to be in one place for a while."

*   *   *

Mia

When we got home, Grandma gave me the stuffed bear. I smiled and said, "Thank you," although I was still having trouble getting used to how old Grandma looked. She looked almost as old as Tai Po had looked when I had seen her last. This reminded me that I had recently overheard Mom and Dad talking about Tai Po. They had said that she was very ill and might not live much longer. This scared me.

As I was kneeling to say my prayers that night, I asked Mom, "Is Grandma going to die soon?"

She reached over to pull me close as she answered, "I cannot predict when someone will die. As far as I know, Grandma is healthy. Why are you asking?"

"I know when people get old, they die. Grandma looks so old. I am glad she is healthy. I don't want Grandma to die."

"I don't think Grandma will die anytime soon."

"Thanks, Mommy. I'm going to say a prayer for Grandma to live a long time."

Francesca

The next day, I reminded Mia that I would be picking up Auntie Angie and Uncle Dave along with their four-month-old, Alex, from the airport while she was at school. I was excited to see them; however, I could tell that Mia had mixed feelings.

Mia

I did feel better about Grandma after talking to Mom, but it was still strange to see all of the extra lines on Grandma's face. I was also concerned about having another baby in the house. Babies just took all of the attention away from me.

At the end of the school day, Auntie Angie walked through the classroom door with Mom.

"Mia, look how you've grown. I need to visit more often or I will not recognize you next time. Can I have a hug from my adorable niece?"

"Auntie Angie!" I said as I hugged her, realizing that she did not have a baby with her. Then I turned to Mom as we walked to our van. "Where's Cal?"

Francesca
As I opened the back door so Mia could climb in, I said, "He's at home with Grandma, Auntie Flora, Uncle Dave, and Alex. Alex was taking a nap so Uncle Dave offered to watch Cal as well."

Mia's face dropped as I buckled her into her booster seat.

"Oh, I thought Auntie Angie decided to come by herself."

Angie turned around in the front passenger seat with one eyebrow raised.

As I started to close the back door, I told Angie, "I think Mia just has a problem sharing the limelight with babies in general."

As I entered through the driver's door, I heard Mia ask, "I've never seen a light that is lime colored, so why would I care about sharing it?"

Mia
Auntie Angie and Mom both laughed before Auntie Angie said, "Mia, don't worry. Alex still sleeps most of the time, so he won't take attention away from you."

"That's a relief. Cal woke up all the time when he was a baby," I told Auntie Angie.

Auntie Angie said, "Yes, I'm lucky. Alex sleeps all night and still takes long naps."

I felt much better on the drive home. I really did love my Auntie Angie.

Francesca
The next day was Mia's Christmas program. Ben's parents came with us, and we all sat in the front row. Her class sang, "We Wish You a Merry Christmas" for their last song. Mia was the only one who knew all of the words for the second verse. She was also the only one who sang in tune. She had perfect pitch even then, which is very unusual for a three-year-old. Perfect or near-perfect pitch can also be a trait of Asperger's.

Mia
Everyone clapped and clapped when I finished singing. After the performance, Grandma and Ah Ma both said that I was the only one who sang in tune. I

did not know what they meant. I thought I was the one who sounded different from everyone else.

*   *   *

During my break, we drove all around the island to show Grandma, Auntie Flora, Auntie Angie, and Uncle Dave the sights. First, we drove east. Mom played tour guide. She pointed to Hanauma Bay, the marine preserve, as the best place on the island to snorkel and to see sea turtles, which she explained were protected so you couldn't get too close. They all kept talking about the turquoise and aqua colors of the ocean.

Next we headed inland on Kalanianaole Highway into Waimanalo and then toward Kaneohe. We stopped at Valley of the Temples so they could see the Byodo-In temple. Mom parked the car, and as we got out, I heard oohs and ahhs. This was just for the mountains not the temple because they really hadn't seen it yet since Mom parked down a ways from the entrance.

Baby Alex was still sleeping, so Auntie Angie woke him up so she could change his diaper. Then she took a baby sling out of the back of the car and put Alex in it so she could use her blanket wrap and discretely feed him.

Auntie Angie said, "I can still walk while I'm feeding Alex. Let's go."

Uncle Dave took two strollers out of the back. Mom placed Cal in one stroller and gave him his sippy cup. Uncle Dave put Alex's diaper bag in the other stroller and then got Grandma's walker out for her. We were finally on our way.

As we entered the path, I heard more oohs and ahhs as they saw the red temple with the pointy black roof with the mountains behind it and the koi pond surrounding it. I had been here before so the temple itself wasn't a big deal for me. I was looking forward to feeding the koi fish that lived in the pond surrounding the temple.

"Mommy, can I please get food to feed the koi?" I asked.

"Yes, but first, we need to let everyone ring the bell, as it is good luck to do so before entering the temple. I will go with you to get the fish food after that."

Francesca

The bell was huge. I read the sign that said it was a five-foot-high brass bell. We rang it by pulling back on a big wooden log that swings into it. The sound was supposed to cleanse the mind, and maybe it did because somehow the sound was soothing even to Mia. I made a donation for everyone, as this too was customary.

I explained to everyone that they needed to take their shoes off if they went into the temple. I told them that Mia and I had been there three times so we were going to skip the temple and get fish food from the little store next to the temple.

Then I turned to my mom. "Mom, are you feeling okay? There is a bench by the koi pond that is in the shade if you need to rest."

Mom nodded. "Yes, I think that's a good idea. Flora, you can go with Angie and Dave if you wish. I'll wait here so I can watch Mia feed the koi."

Mia

After we purchased the food, we walked to the edge of the pond near where Grandma sat. Cal clapped when he saw the koi coming to get their food. There were so many that when they swam up to get the food, the pond almost seemed to disappear. They came out of the water as I dropped small handfuls of food, and it seemed like they were going to eat out of my hand. Of course, I dropped the food quickly to avoid this.

Grandma said, "You're amazing, Mia! Look at how many fish you just fed. You're so kind to feed them."

The rest of our family joined us just as I dropped the last of the food into the water.

"They're so big," Auntie Angie said. Then she pointed to the railing by the temple. "Mia, did you see the two peacocks up there? They're so pretty."

I said, "Yes, I've heard they bite. They're wild."

"Okay!" Auntie Angie said with raised eyebrows. "I think I'll avoid them then." She turned to face Mom and said, "I think we're all ready to go when you guys are. Mom and Aunt Flora look tired."

When we got back in the car, Mom asked Grandma and Great-Aunt Flora if they needed to go home or if they would be okay if the rest of the tour did not involve much walking. They both said they were okay, so we drove to the North Shore to see the twenty-foot waves. Then, we turned around to head toward home. We made one stop for a quick lunch and then drove home over the Pali Highway only pausing at the lookout long enough for them to see the view from the car.

*　　*　　*

Two days before Christmas, Uncle Kevin and Auntie Renee and Uncle Lester and Auntie Diane came to visit and brought my new cousins, Karl and Chase. Chase was Uncle Kevin and Auntie Renee's little boy, and Karl belonged to Uncle Lester and Auntie Diane.

They stayed with Ah Ma and Ah Gung, but everyone had Christmas Eve dinner with us at our house. As much as I loved them, it was somewhat overwhelming to have so many people in our house.

* * *

"Mia, we did have a houseful for Christmas. I loved it. I hated it that most of our family lived so far away. I had grown up with my cousins, and I saw my aunts and uncles all the time."

* * *

Mia

My Uncle Kevin, Auntie Renee, and Chase left two days after Christmas, but everyone else stayed until after New Year's. I wished I had more time to spend with Uncle Kevin. He was still my favorite uncle.

All Ah Ma could talk about was how excited she was to have all of her grandchildren home. She told us that she and Ah Gung would be going to the mainland in March to spend Easter with my cousins. I kept wondering if this meant that she no longer loved Cal and me.

"Yes," Grandma said to Ah Ma, "it is nice to visit the grandkids. You're lucky that you have two wonderful grandkids here and that the rest are only a five-hour flight away. I wish these two lived closer to me. At least Alex is only a two-and-a-half-hour flight away, and the rest are in North Carolina."

Finally, New Year's Eve came. Everyone was at our house again to see the fireworks. Chinese custom is that you have to burn fireworks to scare away evil spirits.

Since there are people from other Asian cultures in Hawaii who believe the same thing, fireworks are legal, but you can only burn them on certain days. New Year's Eve is the biggest fireworks day in Hawaii; it's even bigger than July Fourth. I can actually stay up past midnight for the biggest display of fireworks. Oh, joy!

Although I had stayed outside the previous year to watch the fireworks and to stomp poppers, the noise from the fireworks hurt my ears this year and the smoke burned my eyes, so I stayed inside to watch. Because Karl was afraid of the fireworks, he and Auntie Diane stayed inside too. Even though I was inside, I still covered my ears every time someone lit the fuse. Cal was now old enough to walk, so he was outside having fun stomping on poppers with Ah Ma.

Grandma and Auntie Flora decided to stay inside with me. They said that they had never seen so much smoke. They treated me like a smart kid instead of like a baby.

Ah Ma kept saying, "Mia, you're missing all the fun! Look at how much fun your little brother and baby cousin are having. Don't you want to come outside? You can cover your ears when there are loud pops." She said the same thing to Karl.

After Ah Ma went back outside, Grandma leaned over and said, "Mia, I think you're smart to avoid the smoke and noise."

Uncle Dave brought baby Alex in for his bath at 9:30. Then Auntie Angie came in to feed him, and he fell asleep. Uncle Dave stayed inside to listen for him while Auntie Angie went back outside.

Before long, the holidays were over. Everyone returned home. Aside from Cal's occasional crying, our house was quiet again. It was nice.

After Christmas break, Mom had another surprise for me. She and Dad had decided that since most of the kids at my school stayed until 2:30 PM, I should too. This meant that I would have to nap at school again. Mom said that it would be better because when I got home, she and I would have more time together as my nap would be over.

Francesca

It seemed like a good idea at the time because Mia's friends were staying later too. I should have thought about how much trouble she had sleeping at her other preschool.

Mia

Mom just did not understand how hard it was for me to sleep in a room full of people. I could not go to sleep. I did not have my stuffed animal guards to watch over me. I was also afraid that I would accidentally wet the bed in my sleep. Although I rarely did this anymore, my bed at home still had a waterproof pad under the sheet just in case. I was afraid that if I had an accident at school, people would make fun of me.

I did not sleep when nap time came. Instead, I tossed and turned to keep myself awake. I guess this kept some of the other kids awake too. Ms. Nicely moved my cot close to her desk. I am sure she thought this would help. It did not. Now I kicked her desk with my foot to stay awake.

Ms. Nicely tried her best, but she could not get me to stay quiet so she eventually had me go to the office to try to nap. The office person was a woman named Ms. Hardly who was even worse than Ms. Mein was. She scolded me for not sleeping. She thought I was just being a brat. I hated her.

Francesca

I got multiple notes from the teacher during this time. I suggested that Mia just return to half days and go home after lunch. The school discouraged this. They said that Mia would have to learn to nap at school sometime. They thought I was to blame. They told me that I should not let Mia nap at home. I told them that she did not nap at home, but they did not believe me. In fact, Mia did not nap at home unless she was ill, but she would rest quietly in her bed for an hour.

Mia

Mom tried talking to me. She asked that I at least close my eyes and pretend to be asleep during nap time. I told her that I could not do this, as I was afraid of falling off the cot if I closed my eyes. Mom asked if I could sleep on the floor. I told her that I could not sleep on the floor because sometimes kids had accidents on the floor at school.

Mom did not know what else to do, so she went to meet with Ms. Hardly one day just before school was over to see if they could find a better solution.

Francesca

Ms. Hardly did not get up when I walked in, so I sat down in the chair across from her to avoid looking down at her. "Ms. Hardly, I know you are looking out for the entire classroom, and I can respect that. I do have a question though. Why can't Mia look at books quietly while the other children nap?"

She said, "We can't allow this. She should be napping."

"She is not sleeping, and punishing her by making her stay in the office is not helping. Maybe she really does not need a nap. Why can't she just look at books instead?"

"There are children who stay all day and really need their naps," Ms. Hardly said. "If we allow Mia to do this, some of them will want to do it too."

"Okay, so what do you suggest?"

Ms. Hardly said, "Mia has to try to nap in the office for now. When she learns to sleep, she can return to the classroom at nap time."

After this conversation, I talked to Ms. Nicely directly. Ms. Nicely told me that she would be okay with my suggestion. However, she informed me that she had to do what Ms. Hardly said. She said that if I had asked her first, she might have been able to help.

Finally, I had enough of the blame game without helpful solutions. I started looking for another school. I found out that on this island, it is almost impossible to move to another school in the middle of the year. Still, I put Mia on wait lists at two other schools, one of which was five blocks from home. Then, I resolved to proceed with my original solution.

Despite All Saints Preschool and Kindergarten's objections, I told them that I would be picking Mia up after lunch for the rest of the year. They said that they could not refund any money since the semester had already started. I told them it didn't matter.

Mia

That is how I came to be the only three-year-old at All Saints Preschool and Kindergarten to leave school after lunch. Now everyone knew I was different. I hated being different, but I was glad to have more time with Mom again.

I survived my first year at All Saints Preschool and Kindergarten, and Mom let me take off for the summer. We went on picnics again and had fun tossing a ball back and forth and blowing bubbles at the park while Cal napped in his stroller. Cal could sleep anywhere. Mom even bought a double stroller so we could go running with Lightning again. It was the best summer.

Francesca

I could not let Mia go back to a school that was so intolerant. In the middle of July, the school that was closest to our home called to say there was an opening. My mother-in-law watched the kids the next day while I went to tour the school and finalize the paperwork for Mia to start in the fall. I decided that it would be the best solution for Mia. It turned out that this time, I was right.

Mia

All too soon, it was time to return to school, but Mom told me I would not be going back to All Saints Preschool and Kindergarten. Instead, she had enrolled me in a preschool a few blocks from home. Mom took me on a walk to the new school so she could show it to me. It had a big playground with lots of shade. I liked that.

Mom showed me the playground and explained that she and Cal would come over every day at recess to help keep an eye on me and the other kids so she could make sure I was okay. She was also going to volunteer in my classroom one day a week. We walked to my classroom and met my new teacher. Her name was Ms. Kinder. She seemed nice.

The classroom was big with lots of windows. My old classroom had been dark. This was a nice change. Ms. Kinder also told me that if I did not want to nap, I did not have to nap in her classroom. She said that I could look at books quietly instead. I liked that.

When the first day of school came, I was ready. I loved that Mom and Cal were now going to walk me to school. I also loved that because the school was so close, I could sleep an extra half an hour.

The first day of school was a little scary because there were so many kids, but I met a girl named Lei, who lived close to me. Mom talked to Lei's mom that day and learned that they lived on our street just three houses away. They arranged for us to have playdates after school. Our moms also took turns walking us to and from school. Because we spent so much time together, I learned that we had a lot in common. We both liked tea parties and teddy bears. We both had younger siblings. She had a little sister. We both had dogs. We both liked to sing. Life was good.

I should have known it would not last. Mom and Dad informed me that they had put in applications for Dad and Uncle Lester's former school, Manuoku, as well as my Uncle Kevin's former school, Kolea.

Francesca
We explained to Mia that she would be going to a new school in the fall no matter what because she was going to be in kindergarten. We both told her that we would see how things went before a final decision was made about which school was best for her. Mia asked if Lei was going to apply to both schools too.

I talked to Lei's mom, Barbara, and learned that she planned to wait until Lei was in middle school to apply to private school. Lei would go to public school until then.

Mia
I learned I would be going for my first interview the first week of October and my second interview two weeks later. I asked what an interview was. Mom explained that a teacher would meet with just me to ask me some questions and to have me do some schoolwork.

Francesca
Two weeks before her first interview, just after Mia and Cal went to bed, Ben and I were sitting on opposite ends of our comfy beige couch exchanging foot massages when I said, "We need to talk. I'm not sure that I agree with you that Mia needs to go to private school for kindergarten. I hate the thought of her having to make all new friends again. She's always had trouble adjusting to change. Now that she is doing so well, should we really take her away from her only friend?"

"You didn't grow up here so you don't know how bad the schools are. There are schools that have termite damage, and there are schools that have no books. I hear all kinds of horror stories from my patients about how they have to supplement their kids' education. My brothers and I went to private school and so did all of my friends. How would it look if I sent my daughter to public school? Besides, there are only so many entry points to the private schools, and the competition gets tougher in the upper grades."

"Honestly, Barbara grew up here too. She told me that Mia is lucky to have the option, but she is not too worried about our local elementary school. She said it is one of the best. She did acknowledge that part of the reason for this is because the parents are very involved. But I'm involved with her school now."

"I've heard that our local school is good too, so why don't you call to see if you can tour it? You'll need to know more about it if she doesn't get into either of the private schools anyway. Just keep in mind that the middle schools and high schools are not that good and it will be harder to transition at that age, so I think we should still go through the interview process."

I sat up and leaned over to kiss Ben. "Thank you for listening to my side. Your mom just got mad at me when I even suggested looking at the public school."

"Dear, don't be upset! Remember, for Mom, it's all about saving face. How will it look if her first grandchild goes to public school when all of her children went to private school? By the way, I said to look at the public school, but if she gets into one of the private schools, I still think she should go. The kids that come in at fourth and sixth grade are extremely bright."

I stared at Ben with raised brows and a lowered chin. "So is our daughter in case you've forgotten!"

"Don't look at me like that! Of course I know Mia is bright, but why take a risk if we don't have to?"

Mia

I complained to Lei at school the next day that I did not want to have to go to another school. Lei said that our school only went through preschool, and she would be moving to a new school the next year as well. She would be going to kindergarten at the elementary school across the park from our preschool. She said that her mom said that I was lucky to be able to apply to private schools. Lei said that her mom planned to apply to the schools when she reached sixth grade. She said that she would go to Manuoku during the summers until then, so she hoped I got in to Manuoku. We both agreed that no matter what, we would still be friends.

Chapter VIII
PRIVATE SCHOOLS AND FAMILY

Mia
Ah Ma and Ah Gung were very excited about my applications. As October approached, they kept telling me to do my best on the tests. My parents said nothing about tests. Ah Ma and Ah Gung also told me that my dad and my uncles always did so well on their tests. They said that was because my dad and uncles were so smart when they were my age. I wondered if that meant they thought I wasn't as smart. Ah Ma and Ah Gung kept saying that going to the right school was so important. Mom finally told them not to mention it anymore.

For some reason, we saw less of my grandparents in the weeks before the first interview. Mom told me not to worry about anything that Ah Ma and Ah Gung had said. She said that I would meet with a teacher at both schools and that I would have to answer questions and do some schoolwork. She said that some of it might be easy and some of it might be hard. She also said that I would be going back to each school for a Saturday morning group session in a classroom with other kids. One of the sessions would be in early January and the other one would be at the end of January. Mom told me to just do my best.

"Mommy, why do I have to go on a Saturday?" I asked. "Will I have to go on Saturdays next year?"

Mom said, "No, you're only going on Saturday for the evaluation sessions because they're trying to avoid interrupting regular classes for the children currently attending."

Francesca
The day came to go to Manuoku, and I kept Mia home from school because

70

her appointment was early in the morning. Ben even took off for the morning so he could go with us. We all drove to Manuoku, which is about twenty minutes away from our house.

Mia

I already did not like how long it took to get there, and I missed Lei. When we arrived, Mom and Dad walked me to a big desk where Mom told a woman that I was there for my admission testing.

"What?" I said. "Mommy, you said it was an interview …"

"That's just what they call it. You're going to meet with a teacher who will ask you questions and have you do some work, just like I said."

The woman smiled and said, "Mia, it's called a test, but your mother is right about what you'll be doing. Would you come with me please? Your parents and little brother are going to take a tour of the school while they wait for you. They'll meet you back here when we're all done."

I glanced back at Mom. She nodded, so I kept following the woman. I do not remember her name. I was too busy worrying about the word *testing* to listen when she introduced herself. We went to a little room that had a table with paper and a pencil on one side of the room. There was a play area with blocks on the other side of the room. Another woman was sitting at the table waiting for me. She said that her name was Ms. Wong. She had me play with blocks while she asked me questions, including questions about what I was making.

I replied, "Oh, was I supposed to be making something?"

"Not necessarily, but most kids do like to make things," Ms. Wong said. "Why don't you work on a puzzle now?"

"I love puzzles," I said, and I quickly completed the one in front of me.

"I can tell," replied Ms. Wong. "Now I need you to circle the correct answers to some picture questions."

Next, she showed me pictures that looked like someone had spilled ink all over the page. She asked what I saw when I looked at the page. I was confused and asked her, "Can't you see the big blob of ink?"

She laughed at this. Then she said, "Okay, but use your imagination and tell me what the ink blob looks like."

Finally, Ms. Wong asked me to draw a picture of my family. She noticed my picture only had three people. She asked, "Don't you have a little brother?"

I said, "Yes." Then I pointed to my brother between Mommy and Daddy in the picture.

Ms. Wong said, "Mia, what about you? Where are you in the picture?"

I said, "Oh, I'm still drawing," but I really hadn't planned to draw myself.

Before long, it was time to go. Mom, Dad, and Cal were waiting for me. I was so happy to be leaving.

As we walked outside, I said, "Mommy, can I go to my school now?"

"Of course you can, Mia," Mom said as we walked to the car. "Did you have fun at Manuoku?"

"No."

Dad opened the car door for me to climb into my booster seat and said, "Some of it must have been fun. What did you do?"

I said, "No, Daddy, it wasn't. I had to tell them what I saw in a picture of black ink."

Dad laughed. "What did you see?"

"I saw a big blob of ink. I asked her if she saw it too. She laughed and told me to use my imagination."

Mom asked, "Mia did you like anything about your time at Manuoku?"

"I liked doing the puzzles."

Dad asked, "Didn't you like anything else?"

"Daddy, the morning wasn't very fun."

"Mia, don't worry about it," Mom said. "If you're meant to go to Manuoku, it will all work out."

"Mommy, I really don't think I want to go to Manuoku."

Mom asked, "Why?"

"The two ladies reminded me of Ms. Hardly and Ms. Mein."

Mom and Dad looked at each other. Finally, Mom asked, "How did they remind you of Ms. Hardly and Ms. Mein?"

"It was just a feeling that I got. I can't explain it."

By this time, we were pulling into my school parking lot. Dad said, "Mia, we can talk more about this later. Francesca, do you want me to wait for you or do you and Cal want to walk home after you take Mia to her class?"

"You need to get to work," Mom said. "Cal and I will walk home. Okay, Mia, get your backpack while I get Cal's stroller. Let's get you to school."

It was so nice to be back at my school with my friends and with Ms. Kinder. I really liked her. When I first got back to school, she said, "Welcome, Mia. We're so glad you're here."

I was glad that I was there too.

The next week was good because neither of my parents discussed Manuoku or Kolea. Lei and I spent every day together. I was happy.

Then Mom reminded me that I would have to miss a morning of school again to visit Kolea.

Mom said, "Mia, the teachers at Kolea must be nice. Look how well Uncle Kevin turned out."

"Mommy, I think Uncle Kevin was born nice."

"You're very smart to know that. I do hope you'll keep an open mind about Kolea though."

"Mommy, how do I open my mind? It's in my head, right? Is there a door?"

Mom laughed. "Mia, it's an expression. There is no real door. It just means that you need to give the school a chance. Maybe you'll like it."

"Mommy, I'll try, but if I have to go to a private school, I would rather go to Manuoku so I can at least be with Lei during the summers."

"Mia, the schools will determine if they have a place for you. We cannot just pick Manuoku. Maybe Lei's mom will consider sending her to Kolea if you go there. We can talk to her if you get into Kolea. Don't worry about it yet."

The next day, Mommy, Cal, and I went to Kolea. Cal was two and a half, but Mommy still had not sent him to school. She said that Cal had friends to play with in our neighborhood so he did not have to go to school yet. I knew he had friends he played with every day, including Lei's little sister, but it did not seem fair.

Dad did not go this time. Does that tell you his preference?

We went to an office to check in as we had done at Manuoku. However, this time, we waited outside the office for someone to call my name. A nice woman came to get me. She handed Mom a paper to fill out while she waited. She asked Cal if he was applying too. I told her that Cal was too young. She smiled at me and asked me to follow her down a long hallway to another office. There was another nice woman waiting for me. We played games together and talked. It was almost fun, but I could tell that some of the questions were similar to Manuoku's questions. At least she did not ask me to look at spilled ink. I liked this school better. When I finished, they did not make me draw my family. Instead, they gave me a pencil.

Francesca

Mia came out of her interview smiling. I thought that was a good sign. The woman said that she did well, and then she turned to Mia.

"Mia, it was very nice to meet you. You will get to see the classrooms with the other kids your age when you come back in January. I hope you like it. You really did very well today."

"Thank you. I hope that I like it too."

Once I had Mia and Cal loaded in the car, I asked, "Mia did you like Kolea?"

"I only saw one room," Mia said. "The woman was nice though. The questions were easier too."

"That's good," I said as I drove toward Mia's school.

"Mommy, how come it's taking so long to get back to school?"

"Kolea is a little farther away from your current school."

"Oh, so I would be farther away from Lei and I would have to get up earlier if I went to Kolea?" Mia asked.

"Yes, I guess you would have to get up earlier."

"I don't think I would like that."

"You would adjust, but don't worry about it right now. You'll go back to Manuoku in early January and back to Kolea the last weekend in January. Then, they will make a decision in late April and let us know if they have room for you. We will have time to discuss all of your concerns then."

"Okay, Mommy."

Mia

The rest of the drive to school was quiet. At least Mom was not forcing me to answer more questions about the tests this time. Once again, Ms. Kinder was so nice when I got to school.

The next few weeks flew by. I started piano lessons, which I loved. Now I could sing to my own music. I could feel the music, but I didn't tell Mom this because I wasn't sure she would believe me. I could even tell when I played a note that didn't sound right. My music teacher, Mr. Wang, told me that I had a good ear. He taught me to play "Jingle Bells" for Christmas. I even did a concert for Mommy and Daddy at his studio the week before Christmas.

Five days later, Auntie Angie, Uncle Dave, and Alex came for Christmas, and they brought Grandma with them. She was really old this time. I really noticed the difference when Ah Ma and Ah Gung came over Christmas Eve for lunch. We had our celebration at lunchtime Christmas Eve because Ah Ma and Ah Gung were flying to California to visit my uncles and their families that evening, so they would be there on Christmas morning.

I was afraid that Grandma would die during her visit. I could not sleep for worrying about her.

Francesca

I did not know that Mia thought that way. Even I noticed how much my mom had aged, but I also knew there was much more going on. Mom had just had a CT scan of her brain two weeks before the trip because she was having problems with headaches and memory lapses. The results were inconclusive, so they did an MRI five days before she left home. Because her blood pressure was okay, her headaches were better, and the MRI ruled out an active bleed, the doctor agreed to let her travel. She had a follow-up appointment scheduled for the day after she returned home.

Angie and I sat at the dinner table sipping wine after everyone else was asleep the night after Christmas.

Angie was frowning as she asked, "Francesca, have you noticed how much Mom has aged? She seems to be forgetting more things too. Brenda said that she thinks Mom needs to move in with them or to an assisted living home. What do you think?"

I felt a lump in my throat as I swallowed my wine and put my glass down. "Are you assuming the memory lapses are from dementia or Alzheimer's, and if so, how can Brenda take care of Mom? Both she and Brad work, and Jenny is only five and a half."

"I don't know," Angie said as she shook her head. "But Mom was refusing to look at assisted living homes initially. After I talked to her, she did agree to go with Dave and me to look at some when we take her home.

"Mom refuses to leave North Carolina, so that leaves you and me out. Paul and George mean well, but they're not very good with this sort of thing. Do you have any other ideas?"

I shook my head and said, "I wish I did. Angie, I'm worried too. It's not just Mom's memory. She looks ill."

"Yes, I know. I guess we'll know more after her upcoming doctor's appointment. Mom signed a form allowing all of us kids to talk to her doctors, including you and Ben. I was hoping Ben could talk to her doctor and find out what's wrong before then."

"I'll ask him," I said. "Will Mom listen to us even if there is something wrong?"

"She might not listen to us, but I think she'll listen to Ben. She tells everyone about her son-in-law, the doctor."

"Okay, I'll talk to Ben. Do you have a phone number for her doctor?"

Angie reached into her pocket and pulled out a business card. "Here it is," she said as she handed it to me.

The next morning as Ben was shaving, I told him what Angie had said and gave him the name and number of Mom's doctor. After he finished getting ready for work, he called Mom's doctor. The news was not good. Mom had a brain tumor. Because it was located near her brain stem, it was inoperable. She probably had six months to live at the most.

As I stood in the living room crying on Ben's shoulder, Angie walked in and asked, "How bad is the news?"

I turned to Angie with open arms so I could hug her as I told her the news.

Then with tears running down her cheeks, she asked, "Should we tell her or wait until after she gets home to let her doctor tell her?"

Ben said, "If it were me, I would want to know, and knowing your mom, I think she would too."

Angie and I both nodded as we held each other and cried.

Just then, Dave entered the room, and we told him the news. He quickly walked to Angie so he could hug her too. He agreed that we should tell Mom, but he added that he did not think the kids needed to know yet. We all nodded our agreement.

After I dried my tears, I went to see if Mom was up so we could all talk before the kids woke up. She was just coming out of the guest bedroom, so I put my finger to my lips as I whispered, "The kids are still sleeping," and motioned for her to follow me down the hall to the living room.

She looked from one to the other of us and asked, "What's wrong?"

Ben gently took Mom's hand and guided her to sit by me on the couch. Once she was seated, he patted her hand and said, "Mama Allen, I just got off the phone with Dr. Johnson. The news is not good."

Mom gasped and said, "I need to hear it, Ben, so please be honest with me."

He said in a low voice, "You have a brain tumor. That's why you have been forgetting things."

I hugged my mother as I felt the tears roll down my cheeks. Angie got up to hug her too.

Mom said, "Girls, I don't want my grandchildren to see us like this. We have to pull it together." Then she looked up at Ben who had gotten up to make room for Angie. "Please get us some coffee, and then you need to go to work as planned. We're going to sit here and have a good cry. Then we're going to dry our tears and try to be happy for the rest of the holidays for Mia, Cal, and Alex's sake." Mom then looked at Dave. "Be a dear and help Ben please."

I asked Mom to stay with us so Ben could direct her care, but she wanted to go home. She wanted to see the other grandkids and the rest of her kids. She decided that after this trip, she would move in with Brenda for as long as it was safe for her to be there. Angie and Dave would still take her to look at some assisted living places when she got home.

Mia was out of school for the week after Christmas so she could spend time with Mom, Angie, and David. I also took lots of video and pictures. Mia missed school, but she seemed to enjoy the time with Grandma. They had become close when Grandpa died, but now they were even closer. Even Angie commented on it. Of course, she was getting to know Mia better as well. Mia had just started piano lessons two months before, and she played "Pop Goes the Weasel" for Grandma, Auntie Angie, and Uncle David. They all clapped. Mia bowed.

Mia

I could tell something was wrong with Grandma, but no one told me anything, and I didn't ask because I wasn't sure I wanted to know. I wanted to make her feel better. I liked seeing Grandma smile; that was why I played for her. She was so happy. She told me that she remembered all of her children, including Mom, playing that song over the years on various instruments.

Auntie Angie and Uncle Dave were also fun. They played catch with me in the backyard. They also let me blow bubbles for Cal and Alex to chase. Even though Alex was now walking, he did not get into any of my things because he was too busy playing with Cal.

On New Year's Eve, Uncle Dave took an afternoon nap with Alex. Mom and Dad had gone to the store, and Auntie Angie was on babysitting duty. Since Cal and Grandma were napping too, it was just the two of us. As we sat in the living room, she said, "Mia, did I ever tell you about the pony your mother had when she was younger?"

I said, "No. Tell me please."

"When your mother was about eight, she and Uncle Paul had the pony by the porch. That pony walked up the concrete steps right onto our porch. Grandma initially screamed to get the pony off the porch, but then he nosed her and Grandma's heart melted, and after that, the pony was allowed on the porch anytime your mom had him out of the pasture. Your mom and Uncle Paul always were able to convince Grandma and Grandpa to do anything for animals. I don't know how they did it. Maybe it was because Grandma and Grandpa had a soft spot for animals too."

I said, "Mom won't even let me have a pony."

Auntie Angie hugged me as she said, "I think that has something to do with the fact that you live in the city, and there are laws about having big animals in your backyard."

"Oh!"

"Besides, having horses had some downsides too. We all had to clean out the stalls in the barn, and believe me, that wasn't fun. It was dirty, smelly work," Auntie Angie said as she held her nose to make her point.

"Yuck! How did you do it?" I asked.

"We wore boots. We had a wheelbarrow that we shoveled the horse manure into before we rolled it out to another area of the pasture to dry. The only really bad part was the smell. Grandpa said it was part of owning horses. He always taught us that we had to take the bad with the good," Auntie Angie said.

"I want the good parts," I said. "Someone else can have the bad."

"Life doesn't work like that, Mia. It would be hard to find someone to do all of the dirty work while you got all of the rewards. Since I've grown up, I've learned that a lot of the lessons Grandpa taught us with our horses apply to all aspects of life."

"Like what else?" I asked.

"Like Grandpa's favorite when he was teaching us to ride. He said, 'When you fall off a horse, you have to get back on.'"

"Yeah, but I don't have a horse," I said as I gave my auntie a puzzled look.

"Mia, it's a very old saying, but it applies to anything in life. It's another way of saying, 'If first you don't succeed, try, try again,'" Auntie Angie said.

I shook my head and threw up my hands as I said, "I don't understand."

"Okay, let me put it in preschool terms," Auntie Angie said as she picked up one of Cal's board books. "Do you remember the story *The Little Engine That Could*?"

"Yes, Mommy reads it to Cal all the time," I said. "It's one of his favorites."

"Well, that story is about not giving up just because you can't do something the first time. You have to keep trying and believe in yourself," she said as she put the book down. "That's really all the saying about getting back on the horse is about."

"Okay," I said just as Mom and Dad got home.

"Let's go help your parents bring in the groceries," Auntie Angie said as she got off the couch and held out her hand for me.

The best things about New Year's Eve were the sparkling apple cider and mochi, both of which were a tradition at our house. I still hated the fireworks though. Grandma stayed in with me and asked me to play another song for her on my piano. I told her that I didn't know any other songs well enough to play them except for "Jingle Bells." She said to play that, so I did. Even though it was after Christmas, Grandma clapped.

The day after New Year's, we drove Grandma, Auntie Angie, Uncle Dave, and Alex to the airport. I thought Mom was going to cry. I was surprised that she was so sad to see them go. I would miss them, but I was ready to go back to school on Monday to see all of my friends. I thought Mom would be happy to have our house back to ourselves.

Chapter IX
LIFE CHANGES

Francesca

Life resumed as normal for the kids. Mia returned to school, and Cal continued having playdates. But my life would never be the same as I realized how close I was to becoming the senior generation.

It had been hard when Dad died, but Mom was Mom! I could not imagine life without her. Once she died, Aunt Flora would be the only one left from that generation.

I was remembering when I was young how all the aunts, uncles, and cousins got together every weekend until my grandma died and how we still got together on holidays after that. My children did not get to grow up with that experience. And now they would have to live the rest of their years without maternal grandparents.

When Mom went home, they did a brain biopsy to stage her tumor, which we already knew was inoperable because it extended from her temporal lobe down to her brain stem. The biopsy showed it was a stage IV glioblastoma multiforme tumor. Mom listened to her limited treatment options and decided that an extra three months of life was neither worth the expense nor the side effects it would cause. She decided to accept hospice instead.

Ben and I had made plans to take the kids to visit Mom for Easter, but after Mom's biopsy and subsequent decision, I knew I couldn't wait that long.

I talked to her doctors and did my research. Too many thoughts were going through my head.

Mom might not live until Easter, and if she does, she might lose more of her memory before she dies. There is a chance that the tumor will affect her central nervous system and make her immobile, or worse, cause her to slip into a coma before I make it home. I should be there while she can still remember me. My kids need to spend as much time with their grandma as they can while there is still time left. I'm letting them all down. Being so far away is awful!

Finally, I told Ben that I needed to go sooner, but that I wanted to be there for Easter too. He agreed. I made plans to travel with the kids the day after Mia's second testing day with Kolea at the end of January. We decided not to tell the kids until after Mia's last testing day. We did not want to worry them. I saw no point when nothing would change.

I spoke to Angie frequently, as I knew that she would understand; of course, she did.

One day, I received a big envelope in the mail from Angie. As I opened it, I saw pictures of what I assumed was an assisted living home, and I read,

> Dear Francesca,
>
> I took Mom to visit several assisted living homes. This was the nicest. After I got Brenda to visit it too, she finally agreed that it was the best option for Mom. With Brenda's blessing, Mom made the hard decision to move next week. The home hospice will visit and treat her there. Call me when you get this.
>
> Love, Angie

I picked up the phone and dialed as I walked toward the back of the house. Angie answered on the second ring. "Hello?"

"Hey, Angie, it's Francesca. I got your note and the pictures today. Thanks so much."

Angie said, "Francesca, you're welcome. I'm glad you got them so fast. I knew you would want to know what the place looked like."

I opened the back door shades as I sat down. "The rooms look big and cheery. I feel better knowing someone is checking on Mom during the day and that they are there if she needs them. I wish I could be there."

Angie's voice was soft as she said, "Mom knows that you have to be there for Mia and Cal. She is actually worried about you. She said that you should never feel guilty for taking care of your kids. She's looking forward to your visit in a few weeks."

I said, "Thanks for telling me. I know she feels that way. Still, it's so hard being so far away. I feel so helpless. I really want my kids to have good memories of her. I want to be there while she is still able to talk and get around."

"I think it's good that she has something to look forward to. At least Mia is old enough to remember her. Cal might have some memories. Alex isn't even eighteen months old; he won't remember her," Angie said as her voice cracked. Then she added, "I should have gotten married earlier and started my family sooner."

"Angie, you know that Mom always told us that we had choices that she didn't. She always said that we should get good educations so we could have good jobs. She never expected us to get married or to have children before we finished our schooling. She didn't know she and Dad would both die before their eightieth birthdays, but I know she still feels the same way. You just finished your doctorate right before Alex was born. You and Dave have only been married two and a half years," I said as I tried to hold back my tears.

Angie was crying now. "I know, but Dad never even got to see Alex, and now Mom is dying before he is old enough to remember her."

As I felt my own face get wet, I gently said, "I think we should all be grateful that at least Dad lived until after your marriage. At least you had Alex while Mom is alive. Dad told me that he was so glad to live to see you happily married. I know Mom feels the same way. I promise I will help you tell your children stories about Mom and Dad. Alex may not remember his time with Grandma, but he'll know her and his Grandpa through us."

"Francesca, can you please remember to follow your own advice?" Angie asked me as she sniffled. "I was there when Dad died. I know how upset you were that he didn't live to see Cal in person."

"Of course I was upset," I said and then blew my nose. "But as Cal grows, I see so much of Dad in him. Did I tell you that he patted my shoulder the other day when I hugged him? Do you remember how Dad always did that? Cal helps me through all of this. He is so much like Dad. He knows all of the names of all of the trains, the big construction equipment, and even different types of tractors already. He would have loved to ride with Dad on his tractor."

"Wait a minute!" Angie gasped. "I seem to remember you driving Dad's tractor when you were younger. You do know that Mom hasn't sold it. Why can't you take him on it? Brenda, George, and Paul said that they're going to wait until we're all home to make decisions about what to sell, and Mom agreed to this."

"Angie, you're right as usual," I said. "I will take him on the tractor and tell him more about Grandpa as he rides on it with me. Thanks again!"

"Thank you too," Angie said. "I know all of our family will tell my kids stories one day. We'll all get through this together."

I heard a whimper from the other room. "Cal is waking up from his nap, and we have to go get Mia soon, so I'll talk to you later."

"All right, just focus on the kids for now. Mia needs to see her strong, confident mom so she can get through her group session tomorrow. I'll talk to you soon."

I was so grateful that I had Angie. I hoped one day Mia and Cal would be as close as we were.

When Cal and I picked Mia up from school, she said, "Mom, guess what! Nick and Jenny said that they would see me tomorrow at Manuoku."

"Mia, that's great!"

"Mom, Nick said that we probably won't be in the same class. He said that he heard that they separate kids that know each other."

"Nick may be right, but I'm sure that you'll still see him there. Just remember, treat tomorrow like a regular class day. Listen to the teachers, and do your best."

"Okay, Mom."

The whole family, including Ben, woke up early the next morning and headed to Manuoku. When we arrived, Mia saw that she would be in the same room as Jenny. This made her feel better. When it was time to go into the classroom, she just waved good-bye.

Ben, Cal, and I went to the auditorium to hear more about Manuoku. Ben already knew most of it since he had gone to school there. The presentation was impressive.

I still had concerns. I knew that most of the kids who went to Manuoku were wealthy. I wanted my children to be down-to-earth, not snobs. I wanted them to appreciate what they had and to learn to pass on their good fortune to those less fortunate. I still did not see how Manuoku would instill these values.

Finally, it was time to pick Mia up from the classroom. This time, she seemed happy. She smiled as she waved good-bye to Jenny when we walked to the car.

As we got in the car, Mia said, "Mom, it was so much fun."

"Mia, I'm glad you had fun," I said as I passed Cal his plastic container of cereal.

As we drove toward home, Mia said, "They read us a story and asked us questions about it. Then we went to the playground. I even tried the monkey bars. I made it halfway across."

"Wow! That's great," Ben said. "Was the teacher nice?"

"I had Ms. Sweetly. She was so nice. She said that she has taught there a long time. Did you have her as a teacher, Daddy? She thinks that it is the best school."

Ben said, "No, I think she came after I was in high school. I agree with her that it is a good school. It's great that you had a good day!"

"Yeah, Daddy, I did. Did Mommy talk to you about the ballet lessons?"

"Ben, I forgot to tell you, Barbara, Lei's Mom, said that Mia can go with them to watch Lei's ballet lesson today. Ballet might be good for Mia, and it will be a way for the girls to still be together if they go to different schools next year."

"Okay, I know when I'm outnumbered," Ben said. "Mia, if you like it, we'll talk about starting lessons."

"Thanks, Daddy."

I was thinking Cal had been quiet too long. Just then, he saw an airplane. "Plane."

We all laughed, and I said, "We thought you were asleep because you were so quiet."

"No, Mommy. I eat O's," Cal said.

Later, while Cal was taking his mid-morning nap and Mia was at Lei's ballet lesson, I talked to Ben as we sat on the living room couch. "I really think this will be good for Mia. She and Lei will still have a way to feel connected. I think it's the perfect choice.

"By the way, when I filled out the forms for both Manuoku and Kolea about what activities Mia does, I put down that she has been taking piano lessons since October and that she plans to start ballet lessons. Didn't you say that they look at the kids' after-school activities? Don't you think ballet and piano lessons go well together?"

"You win," Ben said as he threw up his hands. "If she likes it, she can take lessons."

"Thanks, Love," I said as I hugged Ben. "Barbara is going to bring home the application so Mia can start next week."

"You are sneaky!" Ben said as he shook his pointer finger at me.

"Yes, but you love me. Besides, I'm only sneaky for good things."

Ben chuckled. "Yeah!"

An hour later, the doorbell rang. It was Barbara bringing Mia home. I said, "Barbara thanks so much for taking her. Can you and Lei come in for a few minutes?" I asked as I opened the door. They all stepped in and walked toward the living room.

Mia was beaming; she was so excited that she could not stop talking.

"Mommy, I love ballet. They all move like swans. The teacher said that I can be in the spring recital. I'll get to wear a real tutu and lipstick for the performance."

Ben's eyebrows shot up at the mention of lipstick.

"Ben, don't worry; it's just for the performance and only because they'll be on stage," Barbara told him.

"All right, I surrender," Ben said. "Mia, you can take ballet lessons."

Mia and Lei together shouted, "Yay, yay!" They were dancing around the room. They even took Cal's hands, and he joined in the dance. So did Lightning. He was running around them barking and wagging his tail.

I went to get the camera to take their picture. When I returned, Mia had borrowed a leotard and tights from Lei that Barbara had in their car. The two girls were performing. Mia stopped long enough to hug me. Then she ran to hug Ben. I snapped their picture as they hugged. A few years later, I would cry as I looked at this picture.

A couple of weeks later, we took Mia back to Kolea. This time, they gave us a tour while Mia went to one of the classrooms. The school was much bigger than I realized. I could not imagine my little girl there. I thought that she would get lost.

As we walked around the campus, I told Ben my fears, and he laughed. He said, "Don't you remember, the kindergarten kids are in a separate area and even when they move up to elementary school, they are still separated from the middle school and high school kids. I want her to go to Manuoku, but Kolea would be okay too."

"Okay, but don't you think she is a little young to have to walk up that long hill leading to the kindergarten classes by herself?"

"Francesca, there will be someone at the bottom to direct her, and there will be lots of other kids doing the same thing. She'll be fine," Ben said. We had completed the tour and were waiting outside the kindergarten classrooms for Mia.

"Okay. Ben, I think the teachers are motioning to us that it's time to go back to get Mia."

"Let's go," he said.

Mia was not smiling this time.

"Mia what's wrong?" I asked.

"They asked us to draw an animal. I drew a bird's nest, but I only had time to put one baby bird in the nest before they said that we had to turn our pictures in to the teacher. I didn't get my picture back."

"Mia, you can always draw another picture."

"Yes, but why did the teacher keep my picture? I liked it. I don't want to go to school here. They shouldn't have kept my picture."

Ben tried to help. "Mia, I'll ask if we can get your picture."

Ben turned to one of the volunteers and asked, "Is there a way for us to get my daughter's drawing?"

He replied, "The next group is already with the teachers. I'm sorry. Usually, they give the pictures back at the end. It looks like everyone else has theirs."

Ben turned to Mia. "Mia, did you put your name on your picture?"

"Yes, I did that first."

"Okay. Maybe we can have them send it to us."

We all got in the car. We were on the way home when Mia said, "Daddy, I'm sorry. I missed recess because I was so upset about not being able to finish my picture. Ms. Kinder always lets me finish my pictures during recess. I thought Kolea would let me too. The teacher got mad at me when I tried to ask him. He said that I was supposed to be outside playing now. I was too upset to play. I went in when the bell rang. I might have missed the instructions to pick up our pictures."

Ben gave me a sideways look. I could tell he was worried. He told Mia, "Mia, don't worry about it. Maybe they kept your picture because it was the prettiest."

"No, it wasn't, Daddy!"

"Well, I'm sure I would have loved it."

"Daddy, that's because I'm your daughter."

"Yes, you are. Mia, do you know why I went to Manuoku instead of Kolea?"

"Because you liked it better."

"No. I got upset with the teacher at Kolea too. I did not play with anyone at recess either. Don't worry, Mia. I'm sure Kolea was not the right school for either of us anyway."

"Thanks, Daddy. Will you still try to get my picture back?"

"Of course I will," Ben said as we pulled into our driveway.

After Mia went to play with Lei and while Cal napped, Ben and I sat on the couch in the living room and talked.

"Ben, will they really keep her out of Kolea because she didn't play with the other kids?"

"They probably will, but also because she didn't listen to the directions or she would have known to pick up her picture."

"If that is the way they treat a four-year-old, then I don't want her going there anyway."

"Francesca, the other kids were coached by their parents on what to expect. We were naive. We should have prepared Mia. It's our fault."

"Ben, this is not the end of the world. Even if she goes to public school with Lei, she'll be fine."

"I hope you're right, but I think it's better to get in a private school now. The kids that start at sixth grade are so smart."

"Ben, I don't know if you've noticed, but Mia is smart."

"You're right. Besides, she probably will get into Manuoku. You have enough to worry about right now. There is nothing we can do now anyway. We'll just have to wait for the letters from the schools in April."

Chapter X
LOVE OF FAMILY

Francesca

Sunday morning at the breakfast table, Ben asked, "Are you ready for your trip?"

"I am never ready to fly to the East Coast, especially with the kids. I wish all of the nonstop flights from Hawaii didn't involve flying all night. But, I've almost finished packing, if that's what you're asking. Now, I just have to figure out how to tell Mia and Cal the reason we're going to visit Grandma. I really wish I could avoid this, but they'll see that Mom isn't living at home anymore."

Tears fell down my face. Ben looked like he did not know what to do or say.

I said, "I could really use a hug."

"I'm sorry," Ben said as he got up and reached for me. "You know I'm not very good with family members dying. I love you. I just hate to see you in pain, and I don't know how to help."

"You can help by being strong and by holding my hand while I talk to our children this afternoon once you finish at the hospital. You can also help by continuing to hug me when I need it. You can help by the sound of your voice over the phone when I'm away. I love you, Ben, but you will need to be more supportive this time. Our kids are old enough for this to affect them too," I said.

"Francesca, I'll try," Ben said as he sat back down.

"I know you will."

I did not want to worry Mia and Cal too soon. That was why I put the talk off until three hours before we had to leave. I called the kids to the dining room after Ben got home. Ben held my hand to lend moral support.

Mia

I saw Dad holding Mom's hand. I asked, "Mom, why is Daddy holding your hand? You aren't even crossing the street."

Mom and Dad both laughed.

Mom said, "Mia, I need to tell you and Cal something. Daddy is holding my hand as a show of support. Adults like to have their hands held when they need to tell someone something that is sad."

"What do you need to tell us?" I asked.

Francesca

I looked away for a second to avoid crying and then said, "Mia, Cal, the reason we're going to see Grandma before Easter is because she is very ill. She is too ill to live alone now. She is staying in an assisted living home."

Mia's eyes were wide open, and her eyebrows were raised. She looked confused, and she had questions. First, Mia asked, "What is an assisted living home?"

"It's like an apartment, but there's always someone available to check on you. There's also a large dining room where she can go to eat her meals with other people who live there," Mom explained.

Next, Mia asked, "Can we stay with Grandma?"

"We'll stay at Grandma's house," I said. "Auntie Angie is coming with baby Alex, and they'll stay there too."

Mia asked one more question. "But is there enough room if Grandma is in an apartment?"

I said, "We're not staying with Grandma. There is no room in her apartment. We are staying in her old house."

"It won't be the same without Grandma," Mia said.

"We'll visit her every day, but you need to realize Grandma may be too ill to play with you most days," I explained.

Mia

At this point, Cal started to cry. I glared at him. He always had to have Mom's attention, and when he cried loudly, it hurt my ears.

He was reaching for Mom with his arms raised. She picked him up.

Francesca

Cal was crying so hard he was shaking. As he gasped for air, I picked him up to hug him tight, so I would not start bawling too. I did not want to scare the kids. It was all I could do to speak clearly. Still, Mia looked startled.

Cal looked up at me. "Mommy, Grandma's dying, isn't she? I watched Mr. Rogers, and he talked about grandparents dying."

As tears started to fall down my cheeks, I replied softly, "Yes, Grandma is dying. She has a brain tumor. Mia, come here so I can hug you too."

Somehow, I survived the trip to North Carolina without Ben. Mia had trouble on the trip, as once again she did not sleep, which meant I did not either.

I had no idea how I was going to manage to get the luggage and both kids to the car rental shuttle. Then, just as I pulled the last piece of luggage from the carousel, I spotted Brenda.

"Frankie, I decided to surprise you," Brenda said as she smiled. She hugged me and then bent to hug Mia, who pulled away.

"Brenda, I'm so glad you're here!" I said as Mia stepped behind me.

I turned to Mia, who had a startled look on her face. "Mia, it's okay. It's Auntie Brenda."

Then I turned to Brenda and said, "Mia's school had a police officer talk to the kids last week about not talking to strangers or even letting them get close to you. She hasn't seen you in so long she didn't recognize you." Mia was nodding her agreement.

"I was just thinking how hard it was going to be to get the kids and luggage to the car rental without help."

Brenda laughed. "Didn't you turn your phone on yet? Ben called and left you a voice mail to tell you I was coming."

"No, I forgot to turn the phone on when we landed," I said as I too started to laugh. "It must have something to do with the lack of sleep."

"I didn't think you would be in any shape to drive after an all-night flight with two kids. I called Ben after you left. He canceled the car rental. I'm taking some time off while you're here."

"Brenda, thanks so much! You really are a lifesaver."

Mia asked, "Mom, why did you call her that? Auntie Brenda does not look anything like that candy with a hole in it."

Auntie Brenda laughed. "Mia, it's an expression. Your mom just means that I helped her."

Mia

I wondered, *Why is it that people always say something that means something entirely different? How can Mommy be so sad about Grandma yet still laugh with Auntie Brenda? Why couldn't I cry like Mommy and Cal when Mommy told us about Grandma? I really love my grandma. I don't want her to die. Yet, I cannot cry. Why is it that hugs seem to help Mommy? Mommy's and Grandma's hugs are okay, but I do not like it when other people hug me. I hope I do not have to hug everyone we see.*

Francesca

I secured the kids in the car seats Brenda had borrowed from George and Cindy as she loaded the luggage in the back of her van. Then she drove toward Mom's house, stopping along the way to pick up food. As she drove, Brenda said, "I'm going to leave my van with you if I can get Mom's old car to start. That way, you and Angie will have a vehicle large enough for all of you. Brad will pick up Angie and Alex from the airport tomorrow."

Once we arrived, I showered while the kids ate. Then, after I ate, I got Mia to bathe while Brenda bathed Cal for me and put him down. Mia would not nap unless I agreed to nap with her.

So after I made sure that Mom's car started and that Brenda had left safely, I went to lay down with Mia. I woke up hours later to Mia softly tapping me on the shoulder.

Mia said, "Mommy, it's dark, and I'm scared."

It was late afternoon, and with Mom's curtains, the room was dark. I looked over at Cal and saw that his eyes were open and looking back at me. I said, "I think we slept the whole day. We better get up and see what we can find to eat and try to go see Grandma before it gets too late."

I fed the kids and called Brenda to make sure that I had the right directions.

"I'll meet you there," Brenda promised. "Brad will be home soon to watch Jenny. I should warn you that Mom looks bad. Mia seems really sensitive. If you want to, you can drop the kids off here and Brad can watch them too."

"Thanks for the offer, but I really think Mom is going to want to see her grandchildren. It may be hard for Mia, but she'll be okay. I will explain things to her first."

As I hung up, Mia asked, "Mommy, what do you need to explain to me?"

"Mia, remember how I told you that Grandma is too ill to live alone?"

"Yes."

"Well, Grandma looks ill too, and Auntie Brenda just wants to be sure that you're aware of this. She's concerned that Grandma's appearance will be scary for you. I know Grandma really wants to see you, and I think that you can handle it."

"Mommy, can we call Grandma to talk to her and to let her know that we're coming?" Mia asked. "Maybe, she'll be able to put on makeup before we get there so she will look better."

I smiled at Mia. "We can call first. You need to understand that Grandma may not be able to put on makeup because she may not feel up to it."

"Mommy, I really love Grandma. I want to see her no matter what she looks like," Mia said.

"I know, Mia. Let's call her first anyway. Then she'll know we're on the way."

Mia

I was somewhat scared to see Grandma after talking to Mommy. I did love Grandma, but I really did not like to see people who were so old or sick. I think I was afraid that they would die while I was there. I could not tell Mommy this. I did not want to sound selfish or to make Mommy cry.

When we got to Grandma's room, she did look ill, but she was sitting up in bed and she had on lipstick. I bet she put it on for me. Mom hugged and kissed Grandma. Then Grandma looked at me.

"Mia, come give me a hug," Grandma said. "Seeing you and Cal is the best medicine. I'm so glad you're here. I've missed you."

I hugged Grandma and stepped away so Cal could hug her too. Mom motioned for me to sit on a small brown couch with her.

Francesca

I called Mia over to sit with me so I could give her a hug because she looked a little overwhelmed. Cal just crawled into bed with his grandma. I smiled at him. "Mom, is it okay for Cal to be on your bed?"

"Of course it's okay. Mia can come up here too if she wants."

Mia looked up at her grandma. "Maybe next visit, Grandma. I think the bed would be too crowded right now."

Mia's comment caused Mom to laugh before she responded. "Okay. So tell me all about school."

"Grandma, school is okay except that I have all this work I need to do while I'm here. My teacher gave me twenty worksheets to do. Plus, I have to write in my journal and do my reading."

"Wow, Mia, that is a lot! Four-year-olds did not have to do so much work when your mommy was young."

I laughed. "That's true, but Mia is very capable of doing the work."

Mom said, "I know she is. Mia, I'm so proud of you. You are a smart and beautiful girl. I also heard that your piano and ballet lessons are going well."

"Ballet is so much fun. My friend Lei takes lessons with me so we practice together. Auntie Barbara said that I should practice while I'm here too."

"Mia, can you show me some of your moves now?"

Mia practiced her ballet in front of her grandma almost every day for the rest of our trip. Mom even had enough strength to go to the community center for a few days so that Mia could play the songs she remembered from her piano lessons. The two of them were so close that it brought tears to my eyes.

When we were not visiting Mom, Brenda, Angie, and I were going through Mom's house. We put things in boxes that we knew we should save. We also sorted things into a giveaway box and into a to-sell box.

The cousins played together or napped while we did this. Sometimes we took turns playing outside with them or taking them for a walk. Mia and Cal were getting to explore the area where I grew up. It was nice for them to realize that their mom had played in the same places where they were playing now. I even took them to meet some of the neighbors that I still knew.

Two days after we got there, Angie reminded me about the tractor. We went to the barn. The tractor was still there.

As the barn door opened, Cal let out a big scream of joy. "Mommy, look, a tractor! Can I ride on it?"

I said, "I think that's why Auntie Angie suggested we take a walk to the barn. Let me see if I remember how to drive it and if there is room for you and Mia to sit with me."

I climbed up the tractor and started the motor. I put it in reverse as Angie opened the doors wide for me to get out of the barn. After I had it out of the barn, Angie helped Mia climb up to sit beside me. Then she picked up Cal and handed him to me.

"Have fun!" Angie said.

Cal asked, "What about Alex?"

Angie said, "We'll take a ride after you."

Cal had a wide grin on his face. Mia looked worried.

"Mia, are you okay?" I asked.

"Mommy, where is my seat belt?"

"Mia, tractors don't go very fast so there are no seat belts," I said.

"Mommy are you sure you know how to drive this thing?" Mia asked.

"Yes, Mia, I used to help Grandpa cut the grass with this tractor. I know how to drive it," I reassured Mia.

I drove the kids around Mom's ten acres of land. I think it was the best experience Cal had ever had. He kept saying, "This is so fun!" as he grinned from ear to ear. He pointed to birds that flew by. He said, "I love this! I'm so high up."

I let him sit on my lap for the last few feet so he could pretend to drive while I held the wheel. He was in heaven. He said, "I drove a tractor."

Before I knew it, three weeks had passed. It was time to return to Hawaii. We told Mom good-bye and let her know that we would be back in two months for Easter.

Chapter XI
For Grandma

Francesca

When we went back for Easter, Ben traveled with us. Dave also came with Angie and Alex. Mom was well enough to come home for the day. We were all able to spend one last Easter with Mom. Two days later, she slipped into a coma, never to regain consciousness.

The adults all took turns staying with her until the end. I was glad that we had our time together two months earlier so Mia had more time with Grandma. I knew she would always remember how much her grandma loved her. I was hoping Cal would remember too.

Mia

I woke up in the middle of the night when Grandma died. I had dreamed that Grandma had come by to say good-bye. She said, "Don't be sad, Mia. I will always love you. Grandpa is here with the angels to take me to heaven. Angels will always watch over you, my darling granddaughter."

The phone started ringing as I was trying to make sure that it was really a dream by opening my eyes and by pinching myself. I got out of bed to go hug Mom. I knew it was Dad calling to say Grandma had died.

It had been Dad's turn to stay with Grandma. I found Mom sitting at the kitchen table with tears running down her cheeks. I ran to hug her.

Mom picked me up as she said, "Mia, Grandma just died. She is with the angels now."

I hugged Mom. "Mommy, I know, but she said that Grandpa and the angels were taking her to heaven. She does not want us to be sad. She has gone to heaven to live with Grandpa."

Francesca

I held Mia tight. I knew Mom loved Mia, and I knew despite the physical distance between Hawaii and North Carolina, Mia seemed to have a strong connection to my family. But I didn't realize just how close a bond existed between Mia and Mom until the night Mom died. It did not matter that we lived so far away; they still shared special things. Mia's favorite color was pink and so was her Grandma's. She still treasured her pink bear that Mom and Dad gave her when she was born, and most recently, her favorite stuffed animal was Rosie, the pink bunny Mom had given her when Dad died. Mom was the only one Mia always spoke to on the phone and even wanted to call.

I should not have been surprised that Mom would use my daughter to let me know that she was in heaven with Dad. The funny thing was that Mia was the only one Mom told good-bye. She did not even open her eyes or try to speak to Ben. Even though I was sleeping too, she didn't come to me or to any of my brothers or sisters or nieces or nephews, who were also sleeping when she died.

Still, I cried as Mia said, "Mommy, Grandma seemed so happy to be going with Grandpa. She is out of pain now. Don't cry."

I told Mia, "I'll be fine, I promise. However, right now, I'm crying because I will miss talking to Grandma. I will miss getting to visit her."

"Just like you have missed Grandpa," Mia said.

"That's right, Mia," I said.

Mia

I still did not understand why Mom was sad again. However, all of my aunts and uncles and cousins were sad too. I began to wonder if something was wrong with me. I could not even cry at Grandma's funeral like everyone else.

After we returned to Hawaii, I continued to question why I was the only one who wasn't sad. About a month after the funeral, I was sitting on the living room floor working on a Madeline puzzle while Mom talked on the phone to Auntie Angie. As she blotted her eyes, I realized she must be crying about Grandma. When she got off the phone, I asked, "Mommy is something wrong with me? I still can't cry about Grandma."

She said, "Mia, everyone experiences grief differently."

"But, Mommy, I'm not sad. I'm mad that you and everyone else can't see how happy Grandma was to go with Grandpa."

Francesca

I sat down on the living room floor beside Mia. "I'm glad that Grandma died happy, but our whole family is changed by her death. That's why I'm sad," I said.

"I don't understand," Mia said.

I tried to explain. "Well, for one thing, we're selling the home where my brothers and sisters and I grew up. For another, other than Aunt Flora, there is no one left of Grandma's generation. That means that my siblings and I are now the senior generation."

"But you are still the same people," she said.

"Yes, but once both parents are gone, the entire family dynamic changes," I said.

She asked, "What does that mean?"

"Well, for instance, did you notice how Uncle George and Auntie Brenda were arguing over what should be done with some of Grandma's things the week after her funeral?"

"I didn't understand what that was about," she said.

"George is the oldest, and he thinks that he should now be in charge. Since we are all grown-ups, the rest of us don't agree. This would never have happened if Mom were still here. Uncle George would have done whatever she wanted without questioning her. We have never had power struggles between us because Mom and Dad never allowed it. They always tried to be fair to all of us.

"Hopefully, once we all work through our grief, we'll remember that we're all adults. Then we will be able to have loving family reunions again. Unfortunately, since Auntie Angie and I live so far away, it will be harder now. Once Grandma's house sells, we will not be able to just assume that we have a place to stay when we go to visit. None of my siblings have as much extra room as Grandma did."

Mia tried to understand what I meant by this. "Mommy, does that mean that we won't be going back?" she asked.

Seeing Mia's frowning face, I said, "Of course we'll still visit sometimes. Except that when we visit, we won't be able to stay under the same roof as Auntie Angie and her family. It will be different. I do hope we will still see all of the family at least every two or three years. I hope sometimes they will all come to Hawaii or else that we can meet in Colorado. Maybe they'll even agree to meet somewhere else sometimes."

"Oh, now I see what you mean about things changing."

"Good, now let me see if I can help you finish this puzzle," I said.

Part II

Chapter XII
Trouble Ahead

Francesca

The summer after Mom died, I heard Mia playing something on the piano that I didn't recognize. I called Mr. Wang while she was playing to tell him how thankful I was that he was helping her to advance so quickly with her music.

"Ms. Lung, is that Mia I hear playing the piano?" he asked.

"Yes, she is practicing now," I said. "She sounds amazing, doesn't she?"

He said, "Please hold the phone closer and let me listen for a minute."

When I put the phone back to my ear, I said, "See, she really is doing well thanks to you."

He said, "I've never heard that music. She does sound amazing though. I'll talk to her about it at her next lesson."

At Mia's next lesson, Mr. Wang started helping her with music theory, and later, he showed her how to put her music on paper. He even gave her blank music sheets to get her started. He told me that Mia was composing her own music and he urged us to encourage this.

Mia

Music and Lei were the best parts of that year. I started Manuoku for kindergarten that fall. I missed seeing Lei every day, but some of the girls at Manuoku seemed nice. There was one girl though, named Morgan, who was kind of bossy, but I didn't play with her every day because she hung out with a group of girls who didn't like me. There was another group of girls who did like me, but on the days Morgan was around, they avoided me because she told them I was her friend. Only one of the girls from the nice group was brave enough to just laugh at Morgan and to tell her that I was her friend too.

Nicole was the brave one. She was a spunky, black-haired Chinese girl with a pretty smile. She proved to be a true friend.

By January of my kindergarten school year, I was struggling to keep it together by the end of the day. My mind raced after school because I had to keep it together all day with loud noises from other kids screaming at recess or talking too loud in class and with weird smells from other people's lunches. Also, the classroom lights were too bright. Mom and I argued every day. She insisted that I start homework right after school each day because she knew I needed to relax before bed so I could go to sleep at night. It was always a struggle since she didn't understand and I didn't know how to explain.

All I wanted to do when I got home was sit at the piano and compose my songs. Mom did understand my love of music, and she encouraged this, but only after my homework was done. I also missed Lei, although on the rare days that I didn't have homework or by some miracle I completed my homework, Mom would invite Lei over or take me to see her. Of course, I also saw Lei on weekends during which I complained about how strict Mom had become and how I hated Manuoku.

Lei said, "School is not as much fun this year for me either. I think more work is just part of it. I bet it will be better next year when we are in first grade. My older cousin said kindergarten is hard because it is the first time you have to do real work. At least we'll be together this summer."

I said, "That's right! I forgot you are coming to Manuoku for summer school with me. I'll look forward to that."

I tried to remain positive because Lei was, and it worked until I spent a Sunday in early April with Ah Ma and Ah Gung while Mom and Dad attended a wedding. Cal went to one of his friends' houses, but Lei's family was busy that day. That day led to so many problems.

*   *   *

"Mia, I remember you became a fearful kid who rarely slept after that day. You were even too tired to play the piano most days. I really didn't understand what scared you so bad."

*   *   *

Mia

Ah Ma had found an empty bird's nest and brought it into her house. I think she planned to put it with the collection she had in the living room. She always told me that the other ones she had were fake nests. This one was definitely real. When I freaked out about it being real, Ah Ma told Ah Gung to get rid of it.

Later that day, I was playing in Dad's old room when I saw the bird's nest again. I screamed, and Ah Gung came running into the room.

I pointed to the nest, and he picked it up and said, "But it's only a bird's nest." Then he held it toward me. "It's empty, see? The babies all flew away. I thought you liked birds."

I was crying and shaking my head. Just then, Ah Ma came into the room.

She saw me crying and turned to Ah Gung. She scolded him. "What are you doing? I told you to get rid of that nest! Can't you see Mia is upset?"

Ah Gung shrugged his shoulders and asked, "How was I supposed to know she would come back here and find it? I knew you really wanted it, so I thought I would just put it away until Mia left."

Ah Ma shouted at Ah Gung, "Just take it outside please!"

I was still crying as Ah Ma leaned down and took hold of my shoulders and asked, "Mia, what is scary about the nest? You've always loved birds. I don't understand."

I said, "Baby birds pooped in the nest. Why would you want it in the house? It's gross."

Ah Ma said, "Yes, baby birds may have pooped in the nest, but they aren't there now. The nest is empty, and there's no poop in it. I washed it out and let it dry before I brought it in my house."

"Did you bleach it?" I asked as Ah Ma released my shoulders and I wiped my tears with the back of my hand.

Now Ah Ma scolded me. "Don't be ridiculous!" Ah Ma frowned at me. "It was clean, and anyway, it is outside now."

I asked, "How do you know a baby didn't die in that nest? You found the nest on the ground."

Ah Ma didn't understand my fears. She told me I was being silly. Then she told me to go into the living room to get some tissue to dry my tears.

When Dad came to get me, I was watching a funny TV program to take my mind off the bird's nest. Ah Ma motioned for Dad to follow her to the next room.

She said, "Let Mia finish her show before you take her home."

She didn't know how good my hearing was so she didn't know that I heard her telling Dad about the bird's nest even with a wall between us.

She said, "Ben, I think Mia has too many fears. It's weird. It must be Francesca's fault. None of us ever had this many fears. What is wrong with that wife of yours that Mia is so obsessed with cleaning everything? I still remember how she wouldn't go barefoot at the beach either. You need to intervene before Mia has real problems."

Dad said, "Francesca doesn't cause Mia's fears. She's always tried to get

Mia to interact with nature, and she encouraged her to go barefoot. I do agree Mia's fears seem excessive though."

What is wrong with Dad? Why doesn't he tell Ah Ma that I am right that the nest is unsafe because birds carry diseases? Why isn't he proud of me for knowing this? Why does he call my fears excessive? Why doesn't he tell Ah Ma that she needs to stop blaming Mom for everything she doesn't like about me? How dare she blame my mom for anything!

* * *

When we got home, he told Mom how silly I was, and Mom said she didn't understand either. Mom and Dad both let me down.

"Mia, I'm sorry I let you down. I didn't understand why an empty bird's nest was such a big deal. You used to love birds. You even made Dad get your picture back from Kolea that you drew of a bird's nest when you were four. Dad told me Ah Ma cleaned it, and it wasn't like she was going to use it for food or even touch the nest without washing her hands."

"It was a big deal because bird poop can cause diseases and for all Ah Ma knew, a bird could have died in that nest. She thought washing it out with a garden hose cleaned it enough. As if that wasn't bad enough, Ah Ma told Ah Gung to get rid of it, yet I found it in a different spot in the house. I was only five at the time, and I thought maybe a bird or something brought it back in before Ah Gung admitted putting it there. It was freaky!"

"Mom, don't you remember how I was afraid to go to bed at night? I had nightmares that baby birds were pooping all over Ah Ma's house after I fell asleep, and I woke up screaming."

"I do remember that you were afraid to go to sleep that night, and you woke up screaming for weeks after that. I had to sit with you longer than usual. I didn't know the nightmares and all of your fears were related to that bird's nest. If I had known, I would have told you that if Ah Ma really washed the nest and let it dry completely in the sun, there was a good chance the sun killed any bacteria that was left in the nest anyway. Since I didn't know the cause of your sleep problems, I tried the tough approach of not saying anything and gently walking you back to bed. This time, it didn't work. You and I were both very sleep deprived after three weeks of this."

* * *

Francesca
Finally, I decided we needed help. After we got Cal to bed and Mia to at least stay in her room, I sighed deeply as I plopped down on the couch beside Ben.

I said, "I'm exhausted. We need help. I can't handle this anymore."

Ben looked over at me and said, "I know. I'll call Dr. Haptrick tomorrow to see if we can get an appointment."

I said, "Who?"

Ben said, "She's the child psychologist that many of the schools use. She's supposed to be excellent."

Mia

So I saw Dr. Haptrick, and she suggested getting a sound soother to help me sleep. When this didn't work, Mom and Dad had me see that psychiatrist, Dr. Riddle, who thought I had attention deficit disorder and that I needed to take Ritalin.

One day during recess, Morgan asked me about the deep circles under my eyes. I made the mistake of telling her about having to see a psychiatrist because I couldn't sleep, and I told her Dr. Riddle thought I had attention deficit disorder.

Morgan asked, "Why can't you sleep?"

I said, "I have nightmares about baby birds pooping all over my Ah Ma's house." Then I told her about the bird's nest.

Morgan laughed.

That was why I never told anyone else, including Lei, about seeing the psychologist or the psychiatrist or about my fears.

I did ask Lei if she had trouble with the tags and seams on some of our ballet tutus.

She said, "No. Why? Do you?"

I was too embarrassed to admit I did, so I said, "No. I was just wondering."

Another time, when she was at our house, I said, "Cal can be so annoying. I can't believe he has the TV that loud!"

Lei said, "I think you're too hard on Cal. The TV isn't that loud."

Her reaction helped me realize that not everyone heard and felt things the way I did, so I didn't mention everything to Lei anymore.

No one seemed to understand, and I couldn't explain it because I didn't really understand either. I wished I knew why I was different, but since I didn't, I was angry with my family and especially with Cal for not understanding.

Francesca

I remember how awful life was then, but I really didn't understand why Mia acted the way she did. Thank God, Angie suggested that we stop the Ritalin since it wasn't working after three weeks. She suggested a combination of lavender and peppermint aromatherapy instead. The aromatherapy with the sound soother finally worked. Still, Mia withdrew from us then. I wanted my adorable, talented daughter back.

Instead of talking to me, Mia argued with me about almost everything from her clothes to food, and she fought with Cal over seemingly insignificant things. The only time she wasn't arguing or fighting was when she went to her room to compose songs on the keyboard she had gotten for her birthday that year.

Mia

The three years from the time I found that nest until the end of third grade were awful. We didn't see all of Mom's family as much then, yet we still talked to all of them. Things had changed even more with Dad's side of the family. Tai Po died in the spring when I was a first-grader. Ah Ma and Ah Gung visited California a lot, and they stayed longer when they went. Uncle Lester and Auntie Diane had twin girls, Leila and Lena, a year and a half earlier. We didn't really know them or their brother, Karl, as they rarely visited.

We'd seen them twice in the last four years. We visited them once when the twins were born, and they came to Hawaii during the summer after I finished second grade. Leila and Lena were only six months old at that time. Chase, Karl, and Cal had just finished kindergarten then. Now they were all finishing first grade. I was about to finish third grade, and I was becoming an accomplished musician.

My piano teacher continued to teach me music theory, and I was still composing. I was also still taking ballet with Lei. Otherwise, life wasn't so good.

Mom was grumpy all the time. She thought I was being a brat when I refused to wear some of the clothes that she bought for me, but some felt like sandpaper rubbing against my skin and others made me itch. I was also very particular about which foods I ate. Some foods made me cringe at the thought of them. I really couldn't help it! Smells also bothered me; for instance, the smell of bleach burned my nose, made me cry, and gave me a headache. I guess it was like Mom felt when she had to cut up an onion. Sometimes, the TV and radio sounded like someone was shouting at me, so I insisted that the volume be turned down.

It was a visit to Auntie Angie's the summer after third grade that ultimately made things better.

Chapter XIII
THE EPIPHANY

Mom talked about going to visit Auntie Angie for months before we went. She was so excited that all of her brothers and sisters and their families would be together for the first time since Grandma's death. I was excited too, because I would get to see Melanie and Jenny. Uncle Kevin and his family were meeting us in Colorado too, since we didn't get to see them very often either.

Unfortunately, after that trip, Mom refused to travel to the mainland again. I knew I was to blame. As usual, I didn't sleep on the plane on the way over, even though it was past my bedtime. When we had a layover in San Francisco, Cal was talking nonstop about how much fun he was going to have with Chase and Alex.

I said, "Cal, I'm really tired. Please be quiet!"

Cal said, "I can talk as much as I want. You're not my boss!"

I lost it and punched him in the arm just as Dad looked at us. Dad grabbed my arm. He had an angry expression, and I pulled loose and ran down the terminal. I knew Cal was Dad's favorite and he would never understand me since I wasn't perfect like he wanted me to be.

Mom was at the coffee shop and saw me running. She left the coffee and charged after me. Luckily, she was fast so she caught me.

"Mia, what are you doing running like that?" she asked as she pulled me to her. "What's wrong? Where are Cal and Dad?"

I told Mom what had happened, but she didn't side with me.

As she gently lifted my chin, she said, "I know you're tired, but you can't hit your brother just because you are annoyed. You should have asked Dad for help. You know better. Running away was dangerous! What if I hadn't seen you? I know you think you're all grown up, but the world can still be dangerous for an eight-year-old."

"Mom, I'm almost nine, and Dad wouldn't have helped," I said with a slightly raised voice and a shrug. Then I added, "He always sides with Cal."

"You're not nine yet, and nine is still too young to be running through a busy airport alone," she said as she hugged me. "I had a feeling that you thought Dad favored Cal. I think you and your dad need to talk when we get to Auntie Angie's. Right now though, you have to go apologize to Dad and Cal so we can continue our trip. Let's go find them."

If Mom had not caught me, I could have gotten lost or worse. I really wasn't thinking clearly. I apologized to Cal and Dad. They both said they forgave me, but I wasn't sure if they really did; and I had lost Mom's trust, so traveling without Dad would no longer be an option.

Francesca

The morning after the airport incident, I talked to Brenda and Angie as we sat at Angie's kitchen table sipping coffee before anyone else got up.

I said, "Help! I'm pulling my hair out."

Brenda asked, "Is it because of the incident at the airport?"

"It's not just that," I said. "Mia seems to be angry all the time lately. She picks a fight with Cal at least once a day over silly things. She's having trouble going to sleep again, and she is impossible to get up in the morning. She didn't sleep on the plane at all on the way here, which is probably part of the reason she acted the way she did. She's always been a good kid, but lately, she has been arguing with me over everything from the clothes I buy her to the smells of some foods and even the smells of household cleaning products."

Angie slapped her forehead. "Oh my! The symptoms you're describing remind me of what a mother of one of my kids with Asperger's syndrome described. It all adds up, especially since Mia never liked to go barefoot and she never liked sand. Why didn't I think of this before? As I remember, she also had trouble with transitions. Didn't it take a long time before she slept in her bed, and then later, wasn't moving to her current bedroom hard for her too? And she's never traveled well. It all adds up, especially if she has sensory issues, which would explain the things you just told me."

"But she's so bright and she has done well in school other than having trouble with her homework in kindergarten. Isn't Asperger's a form of autism?" I asked. "Mia's always had excellent language skills, and she is still friends with Lei, so it isn't like she can't make friends."

"Yes, I know, but I have had patients that have one or two close friends, and language delays are not part of Asperger's. In fact, many of them are smart."

"What should I do? How can I help her?" I asked as tears rolled down my cheeks.

"I think you probably instinctively did many things right, and that is why it didn't occur to me sooner," Angie said as she passed me the box of tissues and leaned over to pat my shoulder. "Mia appears so normal in so many ways. She started ballet when she was young and that helped her with her coordination and balance. You always made sure she was around other kids from a young age, and you encouraged her friendship with Lei and made sure it continued when they went to different schools."

Brenda got up to hug me. "You've been there for Mia all her life. You gave up your career for her," she said as she sat back down. "She's lucky to have you. You'll get through this."

"Yes, but she is still having problems, and I need to know how to help her," I said as I wiped my tears.

"I think you need to take her to a neuropsychologist for an evaluation," Angie said. "I have several good books you can read, and I can get computer programs at cost that might help her to understand social norms, although I think you've already helped her with most of these too. I'll give you advice on how to help with the sensory issues once we determine exactly which issues she has. I only wish I had thought of this when she was younger. I could have saved you so much grief."

"You just started seeing patients with Asperger's a year ago," I said. "None of us had even heard of it until then. I'm so scared for Mia. Will she be able to have a normal life?" I asked as the tears started again.

"One thing I know for sure and that is that my niece is still a smart, talented, and beautiful girl," Angie said as she and Brenda both got up to hug me. "That's what you have to remember. We can help her with the rest. So dry your tears. When you get home, you can find a neuropsychologist and arrange to have her evaluated. In the meantime, I'll let you take some of my books home with you."

Brenda said, "If anyone can handle this, you and Ben can, and at least you have Angie to help. If you need help with any legal issues, I'll help too. Otherwise, I'm here for moral support."

Mia

I enjoyed spending time with Melanie and Jenny. They both liked the same types of music I did, and we all enjoyed playing tag and hide-and-seek with all of our other cousins in Auntie Angie's big backyard.

I noticed Cal was having fun with Chase and Alex too. They laughed about silly things, and when they weren't laughing or joining in our games, they were playing with Alex's toy guns or swords or else tossing a football around. Alex was a year younger than Cal and Chase, but that didn't stop him from keeping up with them.

The best day of the whole trip was when we all piled into three SUVs and drove to Breckenridge for the day. I rode in Auntie Angie and Uncle Dave's car with Melanie, Jenny, and Auntie Brenda and Uncle Brad. We were the lead car. Dad drove the next car, which had Mom, Cal, Chase, and Alex along with Uncle Kevin and Auntie Renee. Uncle George drove the last SUV, which had all of his family and Uncle Paul and Auntie Ann.

On the way up, Auntie Angie asked, "Mia, what types of music do you like?"

I said, "I like rock, I guess."

Auntie Angie turned on the radio. The music playing was seventies rock. She asked, "Is the volume okay for everyone?"

Melanie and Jenny both said, "Yes."

Auntie Brenda asked, "Mia, how about you?"

I said, "I usually listen to my music a little lower to protect my ears."

Jenny and Melanie looked at me with questioning looks, so I explained, "There have been studies that say that our generation is damaging our ears by listening to music at too high of a volume. That's why I'm careful of the volume."

When we arrived in Breckenridge, Auntie Angie pulled into a parking spot at the bottom of an alpine slide. She said, "We're here, girls."

Everyone else pulled in just after us, and we all piled out of our cars. Auntie Angie said, "Listen up, kids. There are safety rules that you all must follow. I'm going to buy tickets while your parents go over the rules with you, then we'll get in line for our first ride once your parents confirm that you all understand the rules."

Mom motioned for me to come to her. Once I did, she said, "Mia and Cal, there will be no racing on the course, and you must maintain a safe distance behind the previous sled. That means you have to be able to operate the brakes. Cal, you may need to ride with me."

Cal protested, "But, *Mom,* Alex said he rode by himself the last time he came."

"We'll see, but if you can't manage the brake, you're riding with me. Is that understood?" Mom asked in her authoritative voice.

Auntie Angie talked Mom into letting Cal ride by himself with the condition that Dad ride in the sled ahead of him and Mom ride in the sled behind him for his first run. Afterward, he got to go down without being sandwiched between them.

The adults each went down once, but all of us kids got to go down the slide three times. I loved the feel of the wind against my cheeks as I flew down the mountain in my sled. It was a blast! Adam and Lisa agreed with me that it was the best part of our vacation. The rest of the cousins liked it too.

We all had so much fun that we even talked to Dad and Mom about going to visit Mom's family in North Carolina for spring break. I noticed Mom didn't readily agree to this though. Instead, she looked at me differently after the airport incident. I wasn't looking forward to going home. School would start in two weeks and I would have homework again.

Francesca

I called Dr. Murray, a neuropsychologist, for an appointment for Mia when we got home. The first available appointment was three weeks away. The week before the appointment, I called Mia into the dining room to talk to her after she got home from school.

"When we were in Colorado, I talked to Auntie Angie about your symptoms. She suggested that we take you for an evaluation to determine what might be causing your sensitive hearing and the problems you have with certain foods and certain clothes," I said as Mia sat down across from me.

"What? No!" Mia screamed as she shook her head. "No more crazy doctors."

I waited for Mia to calm down and then said, "I understand why you don't want to see more doctors, but this doctor is a different type of psychologist. Dr. Murray will see you for three days of testing. Once this is complete, he should be able to give us a more definitive diagnosis. Auntie Angie thinks you may have sensory issues along with problems with transitions. She suggested we get an evaluation so we can determine how to help you. I promise I'll see that you get the help you need this time and not medication that you don't need."

Mia

Once the testing was completed, I was diagnosed as having sensory sensitivity with Asperger's traits. Dr. Murray recommended family therapy to help Mom and Dad and Cal to understand me better so they would be more tolerant of my sensitivities.

I was learning ways to decrease some of my sensitivities, such as helping Mom bake cookies and actually touching the dough and going to the beach and gradually touching the sand for short intervals. I allowed Mom to turn the radio up a little louder in the car as long as it was on a station I liked. I tried new food textures, but there were still some smells I couldn't handle. I used a loofah to bathe to help desensitize my skin. I was also working at becoming a self-advocate so I could cope better and stop taking everything out on my family. It was a long, hard process for all of us.

I thought I might get some time off for good behavior so we could travel to North Carolina during spring break, but Dad couldn't take off and Mom didn't want to travel without him because she didn't trust me yet. When I promised to be good if she would give me a chance, Mom reminded me that there were new airline restrictions that made it hard to travel even if Cal and I got along.

Did I mention terrorists had attacked America after our last trip?

Just when things seemed to be getting better so that Mom was starting to trust me again, my anger escalated the summer before fifth grade.

Chapter XIV
THE WORST OF TIMES

Mia

I got my homeroom assignment for fifth grade in the mail at the end of July, and it was not good. I lost it and reverted back to angry outbursts. That was when Dr. Murray gave me an assignment to answer the following two questions: "Why was I so angry, and why did I take my anger out on Cal?" I was also instructed to add any additional issues my parents might not be fully aware of unless I told them.

I wrote,

> The answers to these two questions are complicated. I'm working hard on my sensory sensitivity, and I'm really trying to learn to cope. Yet, no matter how hard I work, parts of my life just don't improve. I'm not sure if I'll ever fit in anywhere. I just don't get people. They don't try to understand me or anyone else because they are just mean. Even Ah Ma and Ah Gung don't understand me, and at times, it feels like they see me as flawed or at the very least as very immature. Sometimes, I even think they are avoiding me.

> They certainly know my California cousins better than they know me. They talk about my cousins every time they see me. They don't even know what I like anymore. They call me Leila or Lena most of the time. To make matters worse, they treat me as if I am still in preschool. I believe that they believe I am younger than the twins sometimes. Don't they know that I'm about to be a fifth-grader?

> They embarrass me, especially when they treat me like a preschooler

when they come to school events or to my piano recitals. My friends tease me about it. The mean girls really get a laugh out of my pain.

I'm rarely happy during the school year, except on weekends when I take ballet lessons with Lei. We even get to spend the night at each other's houses on Friday sometimes.

There are two things that would help make my life better. One would be if you and Lei's parents let us switch to hip-hop or at least take it too. The other would be if Lei gets into Manuoku for sixth grade. That would really improve my outlook on life!

Until then, I am going to have to deal with a mean group of girls at Manuoku this year. All of the girls in my homeroom belong to the two biggest cliques. One group is okay except that they ignore me. I used to be friends with Morgan, one of the girls in the other group, until I realized how mean she is and how she gets other girls to be mean for her. Since then, I have been trying to get away from her group.

Regarding why I take my anger out on Cal: he goes to Skylark. Everyone there likes him. This includes his teachers and all of the kids. Someone is always calling him to invite him somewhere. He talks about all of his friends and the things that they do constantly.

He doesn't get mad at Ah Ma and Ah Gung when they compare him to Chase and Karl or even when they call him the wrong name. He doesn't seem to notice when they treat him like a baby either.

As if all of the above isn't enough to be mad about, both of you love Skylark even though at the time I was applying to schools, you didn't apply there. Cal's name was placed on a waiting list at Manuoku, and, Mom, you were happy about it. Yet I was practically forced to go to Manuoku just because Dad and Ah Ma and Ah Gung wanted me to go. What is up with that?

Also, I know you don't believe some of the girls at Manuoku are as mean as they are. You think that if I hang out with another group of girls that I have sort of been friends with since kindergarten, everything will be solved. You think that the mean girls are just excluding me. You don't know what they are doing to some of the other girls.

Unfortunately, in fifth grade, I will have all of my classes with my homeroom so I won't be able to totally avoid the mean girls. They are so dense that they aren't even aware that I have been trying to avoid them. I hope I survive the school year!

The only thing I have to look forward to is orchestra. I love music, and I am looking forward to learning to play the cello. I plan to learn as many instruments as possible so one day I can compose a movie score.

Francesca

After Mia did her assignment, Ben and I had our own assignment. We had to respond to Mia.

I wrote,

> I think Dad and I need to rethink how things affect you. We will all continue to work with Dr. Murray and Auntie Angie will continue to give us suggestions on how to help you with your sensory issues. She is also going to send me a computer program to help you with understanding social norms.
>
> We know you're working hard, and you've been doing so much better. You still have to be nicer to all of us, including Cal.
>
> We are starting to understand some of your sensory issues. There are still some things that we think you need to understand. We would like to try to explain them to you.
>
> First, Ah Ma and Ah Gung are not gone all of the time. It just feels that way to you because they are gone when you have time off from school and activities. They travel to California more than they did before Cal was born. They rarely traveled before that because you were the only grandchild then.
>
> This started when your Tai Po needed all of the family to help take care of her. It continued because Lester and Diane had Leila and Lena, and of course your grandparents want to know them too.
>
> Second, Ah Ma and Ah Gung do know Uncle Lester and Auntie Diane's kids better than they know you and Cal. This is because they stay in their house for three to four weeks at a time when they visit. They only see you and Cal for a couple of hours at a time, and they spend part of that time talking with the adults.
>
> Third, you need to remind Ah Ma and Ah Gung that you are ten years old, not three. You also need to realize that when Dad and

your uncles were ten, they were very naive. That is why Ah Ma and Ah Gung really do not know how to treat you. This doesn't mean that they don't know how old you really are. They certainly are not trying to embarrass you.

Now we need to address your issues about Cal. Skylark has a performing arts program, and their teaching style fits Cal better. He has always memorized jingles and lines from TV shows and movies he liked. He has even made movies with his friends. He loves to talk and to make up stories. He wouldn't do well with the rigid academic structure and competition at Manuoku. His talking would have caused him to be in trouble all the time. That is why I was happy that he was wait-listed at Manuoku. His outgoing, creative personality is better suited for Skylark.

His personality is also the reason he has more friends. He nearly always says yes when friends invite him places. He is also more laid back than you are. That is why he doesn't get as upset with Ah Ma and Ah Gung, and since he is younger than you are, he never had their full attention. Having them dote on him is not as important to him.

Having said all of this, you have to know that you and Cal both have good and bad traits just like everyone else in this world. We still think you are a wonderful, amazing, talented girl. We are very proud to call you our daughter.

Finally, how do you expect me to understand about the mean girls unless you tell me? I am here anytime you want to talk and so is your dad. We hope you always know that.

Mia

Fifth grade was as awful as I imagined. The only thing good was that Mom was trying to understand me so I was able to talk to her again.

Most of the girls wore designer clothes to school. Some even carried designer purses and wore high heels. I wished so many times that Manuoku required us to wear uniform T-shirts and athletic shoes like Cal's school did. How could anyone be so girly at age ten?

I still wore athletic shorts with T-shirts and athletic shoes. Mom bought me two books on body changes and on growing up. I read them, but I really didn't want to grow up, especially if it meant that I had to wear scratchy clothes and uncomfortable shoes and deal with other girl issues. Gross!

Some of the girls were already wearing bras. I knew why they carried purses to the bathroom too. They seemed to think it was a good thing. Were they crazy?

As if all of this wasn't bad enough, Morgan and her gang talked about me and made sure they said things loud enough for me to hear, which meant it really sounded loud to me. They made fun of my clothes. They called me gross names. They even blocked the entrance to the girls' bathroom. It reached the point where I begged to stay home for even a sniffle. I hated school!

Things were getting worse. The second day of school after Christmas break, someone left a picture of a dead bird on my desk. It had my name written in red across the top. My friend, Nicole, had seen Morgan write my name on the picture that morning outside of the classrooms. When I confronted Morgan, she admitted doing it.

Then she said, "If you don't stop bothering me, I'm going to make sure everyone knows how weird you are."

The funny thing was I wasn't bothering Morgan, and her friends had already told everyone that I was weird. They even sent some of the boys to talk to me and pretend to like me.

Then they said mean things like, "Do you really think I'm stupid enough to like a weirdo?" as they laughed and walked away.

One day, Morgan was elected student of the month by our fifth-grade teachers. What a joke! She got it because she had the teachers fooled. She brought them presents and held the door open for them as she stuck her tongue out at me. I thought I was going to be sick!

Recently, I talked to Mom about how I didn't have any friends in my homeroom. I also told Mom about how Morgan and her friends pushed another girl, Alisa, when her arms were full so that she sometimes dropped things. They almost made her fall when they pushed her as she was going down the stairs once. Luckily, she was near the bottom step at the time and she caught herself. Mom advised me to offer to go to the teacher with Alisa.

I offered, but Alisa said that she did not think going to the teacher would help because they all liked Morgan. She said, "My mom talked to the teachers last year, and now they treat me even worse. I'm afraid to talk to anyone again."

I decided it was time for me to get Mom's advice, so after I got home from school one Wednesday afternoon, I went to find Mom in the kitchen where she was chopping vegetables.

I said, "Mom, guess who got the student of the month award?"

As Mom turned with the cleaver still in her hand, she said, "Please do not tell me it was Morgan."

"Yes, it was," I said as I nodded my head.

"That just does not sound right," Mom said. Then she added, "Would you like to talk about it?"

"Yes, I would. You have no idea how wrong it is!" I said.

"Let's go sit in the dining room so we can talk," Mom said as she put down the cleaver and washed her hands.

"Okay," I said.

As we pulled out our chairs, Mom asked, "Would you like for me to talk to someone at Manuoku about your concerns relating to this group of girls?"

"No, Mom. It might make things worse. I want to try to handle it myself first. I just need to know who you think I should talk to because I don't really think the teachers will listen to me given that they like Morgan so much."

"How about Mr. Nikula, the school counselor?" Mom asked.

"That's a good idea. I'm going to my room to make some note cards so I remember to mention everything," I said. As I was walking out of the room, I turned to ask, "Will you let me practice what I want to say when I finish?"

"Of course, I will. Have I told you lately how proud I am of you?" she asked.

"Thanks, Mom."

Francesca

After Mia left, I went back to chopping my vegetables. An hour later, just as I was putting dinner in the oven, she came out and gave me a warning.

"I haven't told you everything these girls have done," Mia said in a soft voice as she looked down. "I have to warn you that they've done things to me too. I wrote it all on my note cards so I can tell Mr. Nikula."

"Why didn't you tell me?" I asked as I walked to Mia and gently lifted her chin so she was looking at me.

"I thought you would get mad and make things worse," Mia said as she pulled in her lower lip.

"You know you can always talk to me about things," I said. "Besides, how would my knowing make things worse?"

"I'm not sure, but I know when Alisa's mother got involved, the girls treated her worse," Mia said. "Please promise me that you'll try to let Mr. Nikula handle things before you interfere."

"Okay, I'll try, but I need you to understand that it is my job to protect you."

"Yes, I know. Just please let me practice what I want to say to Mr. Nikula before you comment. I've been practicing in front of my mirror, but I need to know if an adult will take me seriously."

"Okay," I said. "Let me set the oven to go off when our dinner finishes, and then you and I can go to your room so you can practice because Dad is helping Cal with his homework in the dining room."

Mia
After Mom was seated in the chair by my desk, I sat across from her in my other chair holding my note cards in my lap. Then I looked Mom in the eye and started. "Mr. Nikula, do you have a few minutes? I have something I need to talk to you about—Hopefully, he'll say yes since I'm planning to go to school forty-five minutes early to do this. If he doesn't have time, I'll schedule a time to meet with him," I said to Mom before I continued. "I want to talk to you about a group of girls who have been bullying me as well as another girl, Alisa. It has become so bad recently that I no longer like school and I beg my parents to let me stay home almost every day. Morgan is the group leader. She gets the other two girls, Kara and Lisa, to do what she requests. They all call me bad names. They tell other people that I am weird. They make fun of my clothes. They even get the boys to say mean things to me. Recently, Morgan put a picture of a dead bird with my name written across the top in red on my desk. She knows I'm afraid of birds because I told her when we were sort of friends in kindergarten."

Francesca
Mia looked down at her cards as she said the last few sentences to avoid seeing my reaction. As I listened, first I cringed, and then I fumed as I made a fist and tightened my jaw. How could any child be as cruel as these girls? Still, I bit my tongue to let Mia finish as I promised.

"They mistreat Alisa too," Mia said as she looked up again. "They push her when her arms are full, and they almost made her fall down the stairs last week. They keep both of us out of the restroom. I am concerned because they seem to target people who they believe are different," Mia said as she placed a card at the back of her stack and looked at me with determination.

"For instance, I dress differently from most of the girls in my class. This is because I have sensory integration disorder, which I recently discovered. I have not told the girls this, but I did tell Morgan that I might have mild attention deficit. Alisa has told everyone that she has mild attention deficit."

Mia again placed a card at the back of the stack, and then she looked me in the eye and in a strong, clear voice said, "I equate the behavior of these girls to pushing someone in a wheelchair off a cliff. I really hope you agree. I hope you will help me by coming up with a plan of action to teach these girls about how offensive their behavior is," Mia said as she put another card at the back of her stack and looked up again.

"I think allowing Morgan to receive the student of the month award sends the wrong message to our school community. Morgan is only nice to the teachers, not to the other students," Mia said in a firm voice.

Then Mia frowned and said, "I'm finished. What do you think?"

My first instinct was to call the mothers. Then I reminded myself I had promised Mia I would try to let Mr. Nikula handle things first. I took a deep breath before I talked to Mia.

"I think your presentation was excellent. You used a strong, firm voice, and you made eye contact," I said and then added, "I can understand why you thought I would be mad." Then I raised my voice slightly as I said, "I am furious with these girls!" My voice softened as I said, "I am also very proud of you for speaking up when no one else will."

I took Mia's hands in mine as I added, "My first concern is for you. Are you okay? How can I help?"

"Mom, I've seen how the girls respond when parents get involved. Alisa, the girl they push, told her mother. I heard that her mother talked to the teacher. Morgan got very mad and started treating Alisa worse," Mia said with a worried look.

"So it sounds like the teacher didn't give Morgan sufficient consequences for her actions," I said as I gently released Mia's hands.

"All I know is Morgan knew Alisa talked to the teacher. Morgan apparently told the teacher that she was trying to help Alisa by preparing her for high school. Morgan even had her mother talk to the teacher. The teacher told Alisa's mom that Alisa needed to learn to handle things herself. Alisa's mom is now completely out of the picture. Alisa is treated worse than ever."

Mia had her lower lip out as she said this. Then she brought her hands, which she held in a praying position, to her lips and extended them toward me as she added, "Please let me handle it."

"How could they treat either of you worse than they already treat you, and if the teachers believed Morgan was innocent, why did Morgan's mother get involved?" I asked as I shook my head and added, "It just doesn't make sense."

"I'm not sure why Morgan's mother got involved. I think Morgan asked her to help her. She tells people that her mother always believes anything she says," Mia said. Then she added, "Mom, they throw things at Alisa. This started after she reported them. I tried telling Alisa she should report them again. She told me that they are just trying to help her, and it is okay."

I was already furious with these girls. Now I was also horrified at their behavior. I could not imagine a mother believing that doing nothing was best. My heart went out to Alisa. Why would she say anything when her mother listened to the teachers who believed Morgan?

I clinched my fists so hard that my nails left marks, and I realized I had to calm down in order to help Mia. I took a deep breath and said, "I can understand why you don't want me to get involved. It sounds like these girls are already extremely mean. But, if they continue to get away with it, their behavior will only get worse. From what you've told me, it sounds like the teachers are a big part of the problem."

Then I decided to tell Mia about laws that regulate human behavior so she could understand exactly how wrong Morgan's behavior was. I said, "If Morgan were an adult, she could go to jail or we could sue her. There are laws that protect adults from this sort of behavior. Saying hurtful things about others, especially things that are untrue and that cause emotional or physical harm, is against the law. She has created a hostile learning environment. Morgan and the other girls need to learn how serious their behavior is. She should have consequences for her actions."

I added, "Manuoku also has a responsibility to keep the entire student body safe and that includes Alisa and you. I pay to send you to private school so you are safe. I expect Manuoku to stop kids from bullying others. We need to see if Mr. Nikula will give Morgan consequences that teach her how severe her actions are. Hopefully, he will at least listen since we have an advantage Alisa didn't have."

Mia looked confused as she asked, "What advantage?"

"Our advantage is your Auntie Brenda. She isn't licensed to practice in Hawaii, but I'm pretty sure she can help write up something about Manuoku's responsibility to protect you, although hopefully it won't come to that," I said.

"In the meantime, I want you to photocopy your note cards for me. Then I want you to tell Mr. Nikula to call me after you talk to him. Hopefully, he'll be able to help. Right now, I'm going to get our dinner out of the oven so we can eat," I said as I got up and started toward the door.

Mia stood up and grabbed my arm as she pleaded, "Please promise not to talk to the teachers or to Morgan's mom!"

"I will promise that I'll talk to Mr. Nikula first. I will not promise you that I will not talk to Morgan's mom, but I won't call her unless I have no other options. I think I will need to get legal advice from Auntie Brenda before I consider talking to Morgan's mom because I don't think she would listen anyway from what you've said. Besides, if Mr. Nikula can't help, we might consider moving you to a different school."

"No, Mom!" Mia begged. "I have to go to Manuoku. It's what Dad and Ah Ma and Ah Gung always wanted, and I don't want them to see me as a failure. Plus, Lei just found out that she was accepted for next year."

"Manuoku has to protect you. If they will not or cannot help, we have to look at other options. No one should ever have to tolerate abuse. I hope that Mr. Nikula will be able to help after you talk to him. Besides, Barbara would not want Lei to go to a school that tolerates bullies either. I don't really think any good parent would. As to Ah Ma and Ah Gung, they don't get a vote here. I wish I'd never let them talk to you about schools. Your dad might have agreed with them initially, but believe me, he would not want you to be abused either. Now we really need to go eat. Thank God dinner is cooked. Hopefully, it's still warm."

The next day, I stayed home researching bullying on the Internet. I was hoping Mr. Nikula would call me before I picked up Mia from school. He never did. I thought maybe he was just busy and that I would hear from him in the evening.

When I picked Mia up from school, as she got into the car, I asked, "Did you get to talk to Mr. Nikula?"

On the drive home, Mia gave me all the details. "Yes, I talked to him the first thing this morning, and I told him that you wanted him to call you. He called me back into his office at lunchtime. He told me that I must have misinterpreted what I heard the other girls saying. He asked if I still had the picture Morgan was supposed to have placed on my desk. I showed it to him. Then he called Morgan into the office. He asked her if the handwriting was hers and if she placed it on my desk. Morgan admitted that it was her handwriting and that she did it. He told Morgan to apologize, and she did. Afterward, he gave her three days of detention.

"Mr. Nikula asked me to stay afterward. He said that he could meet with me weekly to help me to fit in better. He suggested that as a first assignment, I try to smile more.

"When I got back to the classroom, Morgan was very angry. She told all of the class that she has detention for three days because I got her in trouble. All of the girls were talking about how I was mean and how I can't be trusted."

As I pulled into the driveway, I said, "Mia, now I am angry! I did some research on bullying today. Everything Mr. Nikula did was wrong. He should never have had you confront Morgan, especially if he knew this was not Morgan's first offense."

As we got out of the car, I said, "I found the name of a local police officer online at a Web site about bullying. I'm going to call him tomorrow to see how he suggests handling this."

"I need you to remember the more involved parents get, the meaner Morgan gets," Mia said as we entered the house.

"That's why I'm going to talk to the police officer first tomorrow instead of Manuoku," I said. "I'm going to call Auntie Brenda too. I need advice so I can ensure that you are protected."

Chapter XV
WARRIOR MOM

Francesca

The next morning after I got home from dropping the kids off at school, I called Officer John, who helped with bullying issues in Hawaii. I told him about how Mia was treated.

He said, "Bullying is a problem island-wide. You should ask for a copy of Manuoku's bullying prevention policy. Once you see this, you will have a better idea of how to proceed."

I asked, "What are my options if they don't have a policy?"

He said, "Most schools have some type of policy. Even without a policy, Mr. Nikula needs to get additional training because he handled the situation all wrong."

He told me that the police department had an educational program that they took into the schools. He said that if Manuoku didn't have a program, they could use the police department's program.

After I got off the phone with Officer John, I called Brenda at her office and left a message for her to call me. Then I called Mr. Nikula and left a message for him too.

Brenda was the first to call back. I told her everything Mia had told me.

She raised her voice slightly and said, "My God! Poor Mia! What is wrong with girls these days?"

Then I said, "I think it is our society. I need to know if we have any legal options to ensure that Mia is protected if her school doesn't help us."

Brenda's voice was back to normal as she said, "I'm not sure about Hawaii's laws; some states are passing anti-bullying laws. What Mia is experiencing is a form of harassment. If it continues, the police might be able to press charges against the girls, but usually, they try not to do this when juveniles are involved. Because Mia's diagnosis is on the autism spectrum, she might also have some protection under the Americans with Disabilities Act. I can check into all of this if you like, but if I were you, I would talk to her school first. Hopefully, they'll do the right thing. I'll go ahead and do some research just in case. I'll call you in a couple of days. Hang in there!"

"Thanks! Love you, Sis. Bye."

"Love you too. Bye."

When Mr. Nikula called back that evening, the first thing he said was, "I noticed Mia dresses differently than the other girls. Maybe that is why they pick on her. She also seems to have problems with her posture and with speaking up for herself. I think people would like her better if she were less serious and if she smiled more. I can meet with her once a week to help her with these issues."

I wanted to scream. I was clinching my jaw and making a fist. I mentally counted to five and took a deep breath before I responded.

"Mr. Nikula, I'm sure that you mean well. It's just that I hope you can see that what you just said implies that you think it is Mia's fault that these girls are being mean to her. I know Mia told you that she has sensory integration disorder and that this is why she dresses differently. Dressing like the other girls might not be possible for Mia. As to you thinking she should smile more, would you be able to smile in a hostile work environment?

"Your recommendations give the appearance of condoning Morgan's behavior and blaming Mia for being different. I sincerely hope that is not how you feel."

Mr. Nikula's voice took on a defensive tone. "Ms. Lung, I am trying to help Mia so she won't be mistreated by others. She will need to learn to fit into society better if she wants to be successful in life. I did confront Morgan, and she apologized to Mia. I gave Morgan three days' detention as well. I honestly don't believe Morgan realized that her behavior was wrong."

I was trying really hard not to shout, but I couldn't help raising my voice slightly as I said, "Mr. Nikula, I have a neuropsychologist helping Mia, and my sister is an occupational therapist, who is also giving us advice as to how to help Mia with her sensory issues. I have to say, though, that I see nothing wrong with a ten-year-old girl dressing as Mia does. She still has plenty of time to grow up.

"I am aware that you had Morgan apologize to Mia and that she was given three days of detention. I think you should know that I am also aware that this is not the first time Morgan has been reported for bullying. I believe you met with her last year after Alisa reported a similar situation, so I don't see how you can say she did not realize her behavior was wrong."

There was a pause before Mr. Nikula said, "I did meet with Morgan briefly last year, but that incident was cleared up as her mother and the teachers explained that she was only helping Alisa. There have been no complaints since then."

My next response was anger. Still, I wasn't really shouting as I said, "I see! So if someone reports they are bullied, Manuoku is going to believe the bully over the victim, especially if the bully's parent supports them and the teachers like the suspected bully?"

Now Mr. Nikula's voice rose slightly as he said, "Ms. Lung, you are putting words in my mouth. The fact is, Morgan is well liked by the teachers, and they have never seen any evidence that she is mean."

I took a deep breath and silently said, *Lord, give me strength!* Then I said, "You do realize most bullying doesn't usually happen in front of teachers?"

Mr. Nikula's response was calmly stated, "No one other than Alisa and Mia has complained about Morgan."

I was extremely frustrated now as I asked, "Why would anyone say anything when Morgan had no consequences after Alisa reported her? Mia told me that Alisa is treated worse now than before, and yet the teachers elected Morgan student of the month."

There was a long pause before Mr. Nikula replied in a defensive tone, "I'm not sure what you are getting at, but I can assure you I gave Morgan consequences for what she did to Mia."

"Yes, you gave her three days of detention because she admitted putting the picture on Mia's desk. Then Morgan proceeded to tell everyone that Mia was mean and got her in trouble. You also gave my daughter an assignment to smile more in a hostile environment. Exactly what is Manuoku's policy regarding bullying?" I asked in a stern voice.

"We have a no-tolerance policy. I am just trying to help Mia."

"Okay, exactly what does a no-tolerance policy mean? What are the consequences for bullying, and how are you teaching tolerance of differences?" I calmly asked.

Mr. Nikula hesitated before he said, "That is an individual thing, and in this case, it was three days of detention, and I did talk to Morgan and she apologized."

"I don't really see how three days of detention helps Morgan realize that her behavior is wrong," I said with frustration in my voice. "Today, Mia heard some of the other girls saying that you met longer with Mia. They are saying that even you realize Mia is the real problem, which is what you seem to be implying to me as well, so I would really like to see a copy of Manuoku's policy on bullying.

"I would also like to know if Manuoku has a bully prevention program, and if not, if you would be willing to put one in place. It seems as if Morgan and some of the other students could use some tolerance education."

"Ms. Lung, I am having the teachers keep an eye on things. The students will get some education on tolerance in sixth grade. I really think Morgan is leaving the other girls alone now," Mr. Nikula said.

"I did my own research on bullying, and most bullying takes place when the teachers aren't looking or when they're not around," I said in a firm voice. "Waiting until sixth grade to teach tolerance when children are being mistreated now seems to be too late. My daughter was brave enough to speak to you, and now she is being treated worse by Morgan and by you. I want answers as to how you are going to help make this better. She did not want to go to school today."

"Mia has to attend school."

"Yes, she does, but I'm not sure that Manuoku is the best school for her."

"Where else would she go?"

"She has other options. She is smart. Frankly, the only reason she still is at Manuoku is that she wants to be. My husband is an alumnus, and she has always wanted to attend Manuoku. With that said, I am not willing to pay fifteen thousand dollars a year to have my daughter mistreated."

"I'm not sure what you want me to do. I have already offered to help Mia every week so she will fit in better, and you are angry that I even suggested this. I have the teachers keeping an eye on things. What more can I do?" Mr. Nikula asked with his defensive tone.

"Mr. Nikula, there is a program offered by the Honolulu Police Department that addresses bullying prevention. I would like to see Manuoku institute this program or a similar program."

"Ms. Lung, as I told you, we have a program that is taught in sixth grade."

"Given that these kids are so precocious, I think you need to address this issue sooner. At the very least, you should be meeting with Morgan weekly to give her tolerance training since obviously she needs it."

"We can't do the program in fifth grade because we already have the DARE officer come in fifth grade. We still need to have time to teach our classes."

My frustration level was through the roof as I summarized, "You say you have a no-tolerance policy. You then tell me that you are addressing the problem by meeting with the victim weekly and by giving the bully three days of detention. You seem to think this is sufficient. Have I summed things up correctly?"

"Ms. Lung, you really need to let me handle this. Your job is to make sure Mia attends class," Mr. Nikula said.

"Actually, Mr. Nikula, my job is to protect Mia. My job is not to protect Manuoku. I hope you understand this. I think you and I are done here," I said as I was thinking that I really did need Brenda's help.

I was fuming when I got off the phone. I called Officer John, who suggested that I call the school principal the next day. I told him that Manuoku has a chain of command so I would need to call the vice principal first. I explained that actually he was known to be reasonable.

Ms. Finika was the principal of the elementary school. Mr. Sinclair was the assistant principal. I had heard that Mr. Sinclair was easier to reach and that Ms. Finika preferred he be called first. I let Mia know that I would call Mr. Sinclair the next day hoping this would make her feel better.

The next morning, Mia didn't get out of bed when I called her, so I went to check on her.

"I'm not going to school today. I have a stomachache," Mia said as she rolled away from me and covered her head with the sheet.

I went to find Ben. He was just finishing brushing his teeth. I told him that Mia was complaining of a stomachache.

After he finished, he said, "I'm mad at Manuoku too, but Mia has to go to school. You and I both know she is not really ill. If we let her start staying home, she'll never want to go back to school."

I gave Ben a stern look as I said, "I don't like calling my daughter a liar. What if she really is having a stomachache? She is at that age, and while I would agree with you under normal circumstances, after talking to Mr. Nikula yesterday, I can't blame her for wanting to stay home today." My voice cracked as I added, "There is no one there to help her, and I feel helpless myself right now."

Ben hugged me and said, "You are talking to Mr. Sinclair today, right? It's not like you aren't doing everything possible to protect her."

"Yes, but how do I protect her when the school counselor is so clueless?" I asked.

"Hopefully, Mr. Sinclair will be more helpful," Ben said as he released me. "Go talk to Mia and find out what the story is while I get Cal up, but if she is faking illness to avoid those girls, I really don't think we should encourage this behavior; otherwise, we're teaching her to run from her fears."

"I guess you're right," I said although I still wasn't sure.

I went back to Mia's room and tapped her on the shoulder. As I sat on the side of her bed, I said, "Mia, I need you to wake up so I can talk to you."

Mia groaned. "I don't want to talk. I want to go back to sleep."

"If you really have a stomachache, we need to talk about the reason for it," I said.

"No, we don't," Mia said as she took the sheet off her head. "I don't really have a stomachache. I just don't want to go to school today. Please don't make me," she pleaded with her lip turned down.

"I understand why you want to stay home, but if you stay home to avoid the girls, they'll think they've won. You can't let the bullies win! You're so much better than that. Remember I'm going to talk to Mr. Sinclair today. How will it look if you're out of school when I call him for help?"

"Mom, what if he just blames me like Mr. Nikula did?"

"Mia, people who know Mr. Sinclair think that he is reasonable. I hope that he will be. Either way, I have to try. My job is to protect you."

Mia begged, "Protect me by letting me stay home. I hate school!"

I hugged Mia as I said, "You have to go to school. I'm not sure how we'll get through the next four months if Mr. Sinclair won't help, but I really believe he'll be able to help. If he can't, I'll look at other options. Brenda is still doing research to see if we can force Manuoku to protect you if necessary. I hope it won't be necessary. If things cannot be resolved without a battle, we'll look at other options for next year.

"Right now, you need to get moving so you can get to school on time," I said as I helped Mia to sit up on the side of her bed.

In a defeated voice, she said, "I'll go today, but please pick me up on time and please don't yell at Mr. Sinclair!"

"I promise not to yell, and I'll be there on time, but I want you to promise to try to hold your head high today," I said as I helped Mia to her feet and let her lean on me as I walked her to the bathroom.

Ben offered to take the kids to school so I could call Mr. Sinclair sooner, and I agreed that this was a good idea. There was just one problem. We forgot to tell Mia.

When she finally made it to the breakfast table, I told her the plan. She got angry and slammed one of her schoolbooks onto the table.

Since I knew showing my anger would not help, I clenched my teeth, took a deep breath, and calmly said, "Mia, you do not get to take your anger out on this family. If it is so important that I drive you to school, you can ask nicely."

Mia said, "Mom, please, I don't want to ride with Dad. He always has the radio too loud, and he and Cal talk the whole way to school."

I asked, "Is that asking nicely?"

Mia pleaded in a loud voice, "Please, just give me a break this morning! I'm trying really hard not to scream and run back to my room."

"Ben, I'll take Mia to school, but if you can still take Cal that will help," I said.

Ben raised his eyebrows at me and cocked his head. I shook my head to let him know that now was not the time, and he just said, "Okay, Cal, let's go. Bye, girls." And he and Cal went out the door.

I heard Cal ask Ben, "What was that all about? How come Mia always gets her way?"

I was sure Mia heard it too, but neither of us commented. Then I said, "Let me get my purse and keys from my room and I'll be ready."

When I came back into the dining room, Mia hadn't moved. She again asked, "Can't I just stay home?"

I said, "No, you can't. Now get your shoes on so we can go."

Mia hesitated, and I said, "You have to go to school so stop stalling or you'll be late."

The drive to school was silent. Only when we were pulling into the school driveway did Mia speak.

She said, "Please be here on time after school."

As I stopped the car for her to get out, I said, "I will. Remember to hold your head high. I love you."

"Bye," was Mia's only response before she closed the door.

I felt awful on the twenty-minute drive home. I had just dropped my daughter off at a very unfriendly place. What kind of mother does that? On top of that, Ben wanted to be tough on Mia while I thought we needed to be understanding. How could our parenting styles be so different? What had happened to us?

I knew I had to call Mr. Sinclair the second I got in the door to try to get this resolved, so I picked up the phone on the way to the kitchen where I quickly poured myself a cup of lukewarm coffee and took a bite of half a bagel.

Then I sat down at the kitchen table and dialed. Mr. Sinclair answered right away. I explained the situation to him. I asked him if Manuoku had a program to protect victims of bullying and to prevent bullying.

Mr. Sinclair calmly replied, "We do some teaching about tolerance in sixth grade, but from what you've told me, it sounds like we need to address this now. Mr. Nikula never mentioned the problems the girls were having to me or to Ms. Finika."

I took a sip of my coffee as Mr. Sinclair finished talking, and I said, "I can believe that, so now that you do know, how are you going to handle it?"

Mr. Sinclair didn't miss a beat. He quickly and calmly said, "I'm not sure exactly, but I'm going to talk to Ms. Finika, and we'll make a plan. I will let you know. I would also like you to write a letter with information about how we can help Mia. No child should ever feel unsafe in school. Maybe we can regroup in person in a couple of weeks."

"Mr. Sinclair, I appreciate your help," I said as I tried not to sound as frustrated as I felt. "Honestly though, I think two weeks is too long to wait. Mia hates school, and we had to force her to go today. Something needs to be done sooner."

While he remained calm, Mr. Sinclair's response was firm. "Ms. Lung, I assure you I plan to meet with Ms. Finika this afternoon. I'm sure she will want something done sooner as well. However, I thought two weeks would give you a chance to gather information about how we can help Mia. It will also give us a chance to formulate a plan to teach tolerance to the girls. In the meantime, Mia has to attend school. I will talk to the fifth-grade teachers myself. I will ask that at least one of them be available to monitor the restrooms between classes and at lunchtime."

"Okay, but I hope you know the girls are not going to let the teachers see them being mean," I said with some irritation, although I did believe Mr. Sinclair was sincere in his offer to look into ways to help.

"Yes, I agree, but the teachers can at least try to ensure that Mia is not mistreated around the restrooms and in class," Mr. Sinclair said with sincerity.

"Okay, I appreciate that. I would also like to see Mr. Nikula get more training on sensory issues and on tolerating differences." Then I adamantly added, "I have another request. Since Mr. Nikula obviously does not understand Mia, I really do not want him talking to my daughter anymore."

"I can understand why you feel that way," Mr. Sinclair politely responded before he asked, "Is Mia getting help with her sensory issues?"

"Yes, she has been working with Dr. Murray, and he has given her assignments that she does at home to help with this," I said in a firm voice that I hoped didn't sound defensive. "I also have a sister who is an occupational therapist who works with kids on the autism spectrum. She will be here for three weeks this summer to work with Mia, but I have to tell you that I am particularly offended by Mr. Nikula's suggestion that Mia make all of the changes and that she smile more when she is in a hostile setting."

"I assure you I will inform Mr. Nikula that he is not to meet with Mia anymore," Mr. Sinclair said. He seemed to truly understand. "We will talk again sometime during the next two weeks. You can call me sooner if anything else comes up. Please let Mia know that she can come see me if she has any problems. I will do my best to help her."

I reheated my coffee and called Ben to tell him about my conversation with Mr. Sinclair.

Ben asked, "How are you going to advise them to help Mia when we don't even know how to help her? She is always angry with us."

I took a deep breath and said, "Ben, she is doing her best, and she had been so much better since we learned about her sensory sensitivity until recently."

"I don't know," Ben said, as I felt his disapproval. "She still won't let Cal and me listen to the radio in the mornings."

I understood Ben's frustration, but I also felt he wasn't trying to understand Mia. With a louder voice than I intended, I said, "That's because you listen to a station she hates and you don't try to turn the volume down."

"If I turned it down as low as she wants, I wouldn't be able to hear it," Ben said firmly.

"Why can't you do without the radio for twenty minutes in the morning if it keeps the peace? Can't you and Cal listen after you drop Mia off?" I pleadingly asked.

"You are letting her control our family," Ben said with an accusing tone. "I really don't think it's a good idea."

"Ben, you haven't even tried to read the books I got from Angie and you only attended four sessions with Dr. Murray," I accused. "How can you understand?"

"I'm trying, but it feels like Mia is controlling us, and I don't like it," Ben said.

I tried not to scold or shout as I said, "Ben, just read some of the articles I've printed for you at least. Mia needs our support and understanding, and I need you to be onboard; otherwise, we're on opposite sides."

"Can't you just summarize for me?" Ben pleaded.

"Apparently not, because you don't listen to me. Instead, you accuse me of always giving in to Mia. You need to understand, and I can't explain it to you," I replied angrily.

Ben said in his dismissive tone, "Francesca, I'm sorry, but I've got to go. I've got a patient. We'll talk about this tonight."

When I got off the phone, I went to the living room to grab a box of tissues, as I felt the tears begin to fall. I was fighting for my daughter, and I was losing my husband. I needed help.

After I dried my tears, I sat down in my favorite chair and called Angie to fill her in on my life.

Angie said, "Wow! You are having an awful day. I'm so sorry. Would you like me to talk to Ben when he gets home tonight?" Then in a softer, firmer voice, she added, "Maybe he'll listen to me, but there is one thing I need to say first."

"What is that?" I asked as I felt the other shoe drop.

Angie said in an even softer, more sympathetic voice, "He doesn't understand, but he is right about still setting limits with Mia. She did need to go to school today."

"Okay, so I'm a totally bad person who doesn't understand anyone?" I asked as I tried to hold back the tears.

"I didn't say that, and you know it," Angie accused. "I know this is hard for you, and I wish I were there. You're doing your best, but both you and Ben need to see each other's point of view. I love you both, and I know you still love each other. Somehow, you are both losing focus on that."

I hesitated as I took in what Angie had said, and I tried not to be defensive. I said, "Okay. How are you going to help?"

"I am going to fax over a summary sheet of symptoms and solutions that might help Ben and you to help Mia. It's short, so Ben should be able to find time to read it," Angie said. "I'll call back tonight to talk to Ben too. Maybe I can answer his questions and offer suggestions to help the two of you, if you're still willing to let me help, that is," Angie said questioningly.

"Angie, I'm sorry I got mad, but I feel so alone right now," I said as I felt tears of frustration falling again.

"Sis, you're not alone. You know our family will never let you be alone. Brenda told me she is still looking up information on Mia's legal rights. We're still here for you, and I know once Ben understands more, he'll be more helpful too," Angie said in a supportive voice. "You know your family loves you."

"Yes, I know. I just want to run away from home right now," I said.

"You can daydream about that, but you have to be my strong big sister for my sweet niece," Angie said. "I've got to go, but I'll call you tonight. Hang in there. Love you!"

"Love you too! Bye," I said.

I hung up as Angie said, "Bye."

When I picked Mia up, I could tell she was anxious because she threw her backpack into the car so hard that it almost hit Cal, who was seated across from her. She was frowning at first, and then she glared at Cal when he started to complain loudly about her behavior. "Mom, did you see that? She tried to hit me with her bag. Aren't you going to do something?"

Mia demanded in a loud voice, "Turn the radio off, and make Cal shut up! I don't want to talk right now."

If I hadn't realized how hard the day must have been for her, I would have been really mad. Now I said, "Mia, I'm sure today wasn't fun, but you can't take your frustrations out on your family. Cal, I saw, and thank God she didn't actually hit you. Please just be quiet until we get home. I'll turn the radio off this time. Mia, next time, you'll need to ask nicely."

We rode in silence for the next ten minutes as I silently prayed, *God give me strength! Angels, help!*

We were five minutes away from home when Mia said, "Mom, Mr. Nikula sent me a note today. It said that I would not be meeting with him anymore. Morgan and the rest of her group saw Ms. Fong give me the note. They started laughing. Ms. Fong looked directly at Morgan and asked her what was so funny. Morgan replied, 'Something I was reading.' Yet, I know they were laughing at me. They glared at me, and later, I saw them whispering to some of the other kids and snickering. No one spoke to me today except for Nicole, and I only saw her at lunch."

I hoped I sounded sympathetic as I said, "Mia, I'm sorry that Ms. Fong wasn't more discreet when she gave you the note. At least she did try to address Morgan's inappropriate laughter."

Cal started to say something, and I met his eyes in my rearview mirror to warn him to remain quiet. We were pulling into the driveway by then so Cal held his tongue.

While Mia went to her room to put her things away, Cal followed me into the kitchen to complain. "Mom, so much drama! I know her day was rough, but she almost hit me with that heavy backpack when she got in the car. Why did you let her get away with that?"

I hugged Cal, and then as I got milk out of the fridge, I said, "I'm sorry this isn't fair to you, but for now, I have to cut her some slack. She is going through a very rough time right now, and she didn't actually hit you. I promise I will make it up to you later, and I certainly won't allow her to harm you. For now, it's probably best if you try to avoid her when she is upset," I said as I handed Cal a banana and then poured a glass of milk.

"Can I take my snack to my room please until she calms down?"

I nodded, and he grabbed his things and left before his sister came back out.

When Mia came out of her room to grab a snack, I told Mia about my conversation with Mr. Sinclair and advised her to seek his help during the day if the girls gave her problems. She just nodded and went back to her room.

When Ben came home, he read the information Angie sent and actually listened to her when she called that night.

Afterward, I could tell he was making an effort to be more tolerant of Mia, and I pointed this out to her. Mia also made an effort to be nice to all of us. Yet, Ben and Mia were no longer close. I was grateful that at least they weren't arguing every day anymore.

When I met with Mr. Sinclair two weeks later, I told him, "I'm concerned that Morgan doesn't seem to respect others. Maybe she needs to be taught the importance of this."

He told me that he and Ms. Finika had met with Morgan and her parents and made it clear that Morgan had to learn respect. He also told me that Manuoku was going to use the police department's anti-bullying program and that the DARE program would be put on hold for a few weeks.

I gave him some recommendations as to how Manuoku could help Mia to cope. I learned that her school already taught from parts to whole, which is the best teaching style for kids with Asperger's traits as they have trouble seeing the big picture. The building blocks of learning are taught first, and then the big picture is discussed—for instance, prefixes and suffixes are taught with phonics and then the full word and definition is looked up. The same principle would be repeated with other subjects as well.

To insulate Mia from further bullying, I requested that she have at least one friend or kind acquaintance be in all of her future classes.

After reviewing my written recommendations, Mr. Sinclair agreed to pass them on to Mia's teachers and to remind them that all of this was confidential and was not to be shared with any of the students or their parents. Since Morgan's group picked on kids with known disabilities, this was necessary to protect Mia.

Mia's teachers e-mailed her assignments to me since she was too overwhelmed at the time to accurately hear them. They stopped forcing Mia to maintain eye contact when they were speaking or when she spoke, since this sometimes broke her concentration. For group projects, the teachers assigned the groups and made sure Mia was not with any of the bullies. They also oversaw all of her groups somewhat but not in an obvious way. They checked with me that Mia understood her assignments since I had explained that social phobias might prevent her from asking for help when she didn't understand.

The teachers all followed through on my recommendations, and the police brought their bullying prevention to Manuoku for the last three months of school. Mr. Sinclair promised that in sixth grade, Mia would be with friends. Mia still was not happy when I picked her up, but at least she didn't beg to stay home anymore, so I thought things were better.

Mia

I can't say that Morgan stopped being a mean girl immediately after Mom talked to Mr. Sinclair because this isn't true. She did quit being so open about it though, especially after a new police officer came to Manuoku. He talked about respecting others and respecting ourselves as well as the importance of tolerating differences and defending others from abuse. I know some people listened because they told me afterward that I was right to report Morgan. I wasn't sure that Morgan got it because she was quiet during the class and I still saw the girls being mean to Alisa, but they mostly ignored me.

*   *   *

"Mia, I'm sorry fifth grade was so awful. At least Mr. Sinclair listened when I talked to him, and he promised sixth grade would be better."

*   *   *

Francesca
Brenda did the research as she promised. She learned that Hawaii did not have an anti-bullying law, but that the Americans with Disabilities Act did offer some protection to Mia. That was good to know, although I was glad I didn't have to test her theory.

Chapter XVI
Coping with Life

Mia

After the police officer's bully prevention program was over, the teachers continued to encourage us to tolerate differences. Groups were encouraged to consider being friends with other kids too. The teachers refused to allow cliques to be in the same work groups in class. Everyone was encouraged to support each other and to confront the bullies together. I learned that many other people were tired of the mean girls too.

Surprisingly, Morgan finally learned to respect others. We still weren't friends, and that was okay. I could see she had changed, but the scars of her abuse were too deep for me to forget. Maybe they always would be; I didn't know for sure. What I did know was that the scars were as deep as a third-degree burn. My scars would have required plastic surgery if emotional scars could be seen. I could never hurt someone the way they hurt me. I can't believe that I ever thought Morgan was my friend. She didn't know what friendship meant.

Nicole and several of my classmates thought I should just forgive Morgan and get on with my life. This made me mad, but then Mom reminded me that they didn't know all the details. I was trying hard to get on with my life. I would forgive eventually, but I needed more time, and I wouldn't forget.

If the abuse were physical instead of emotional, no one would ever have suggested that I forgive and forget. The abuse caused an emotional cancer, and Morgan wasn't the only one I needed to forgive. I also had to forgive Dad for not understanding, and I had to forgive Ah Ma and Ah Gung for abandoning me while I was experiencing the worst pain of my life. Plus, I was still angry with them for blaming Mom for my fears and for not accepting or trying to understand my differences.

Mom told me that to completely heal, I would need to forgive others too. This included Mr. Nikula, my teachers, and even Morgan and the rest of the girls in her clique. I really was trying to forgive everyone, but it was very hard to do. Why didn't people support me through this rough phase in my life instead of judging and blaming either Mom or me? Initially, Mom was the only one who even tried to understand.

Dad still got mad at me sometimes and told me I needed a new attitude. This made me feel that he didn't really love me unless I was perfect. Now Mom was angry with both Dad and me because we still weren't getting along. She loved us both, and she hated that we weren't close anymore.

The picture Mom took of Dad and me when I was four now had a prominent place on the shelf in the living room. It was the one of me hugging him right after he agreed to let me take ballet lessons. I think it was supposed to remind us how much we once loved each other. I caught Mom wiping away a tear one day as she looked at it, which made me feel bad because I knew I was causing Mom pain.

Francesca

I couldn't understand why Ben and Mia couldn't just forgive each other. The two of them argued like young siblings who hadn't learned to share. Angie's talk helped some, but it was her three-week visit in June that finally made things tremendously better. She told Mia that her anger was not hurting the people who bullied her. It was hurting the people who loved her. She bought two books on sensory sensitivity that had simple diagrams that explained Mia's sensory issues to Ben so he quit blaming Mia for things that were beyond her control.

Angie also worked with Mia to help reduce some of her sensory sensitivity. She played different types of music and white noise at different levels and had Mia gradually increase the volume of the radio so she could at least tolerate having it at a level Ben and Cal could hear. She also brought different textures of material to turn into washcloths for Mia to use in the shower to help gradually decrease her sense of touch. She gave me shopping lists of different types of food to have Mia try to help her with food issues related to texture, smell, and even tastes. She even gave me more information on aromatherapy to use to help Mia.

She was able to see what I couldn't see, because I was too close to the situation. Angie helped Ben realize that part of his trouble was related to his family's inability to openly express deep emotions. She got him to admit that was the reason he never wanted to talk about his feelings. This prevented him from providing the support I craved. She explained to me that this didn't mean that Ben didn't love deeply, because she knew he did. Because Mia was suffering as a result of our current dynamics, she recommended returning to family therapy.

Mia

Auntie Angie got me to admit that I had overheard Ah Ma blaming Mom for my "weirdness" when I was in kindergarten and that I believed Dad did not defend me or Mom like I thought he should. Also, I told Auntie Angie that I felt that Ah Ma and Ah Gung avoided me because I wasn't perfect.

If I had told Dad any of this, he wouldn't have believed me because he really didn't understand how sensitive my hearing was. When Auntie Angie explained it and told Dad that she had patients who had hypersensitive hearing like me, he believed her. This opened up an ongoing dialogue about what I experienced versus what Dad thought I made up.

Dad was beginning to understand some of my anger at his parents and at him. I was beginning to see his side as well, because Mom pointed out that Dad was raised to respect his parents no matter what. She said Ah Ma was set in her ways and fighting with her about things wouldn't help anyway. He did tell Ah Ma that Mom wasn't the cause of my fears so Mom saw that as progress. Since none of us knew about my sensory issues at the time, Mom said I should give Dad a break. Both Mom and Dad tried to help me instead of getting mad at me. They continued to follow Auntie Angie's recommendations even after she left, like helping me with verbal cues when only family was around and with nonverbal cues when we were out in public or my friends were over. Nicole occasionally came to my house now, and Mom and Dad even let me have a sleepover with both Nicole and Lei. They got along well.

I now had two best friends, and they were both in sixth grade with me as school started. This made it so much easier to go back to school. The teachers were also continuing to encourage students to report bullies. Our counselor, Mr. Nikula, was meeting with Morgan weekly now instead of with me. Although I didn't interact with Morgan, I heard she was nicer to people.

Mom and Dad talked to Ah Ma and Ah Gung so they would understand too, although I still wasn't sure they were really trying. One day, I asked, "Mom, why are Ah Ma and Ah Gung still avoiding me?"

"They don't really know how to express their emotions, so they are hiding their feelings the only way they know how, which is by avoiding them," she said. "Unfortunately, they are avoiding all of us in the process."

"I don't understand them. What is wrong with them? Don't they understand that grandparents are supposed to love and support their grandchildren, not abandon them?" I asked.

Mom said, "They're doing the best they can. You need to give them more time. I do believe they love you."

I was still working on forgiving my dad as well. It was hard since he had a hard time showing his emotions too. But at least we were working on it together instead of avoiding each other.

The nice thing was that Mom and Dad didn't expect me to forgive overnight. They encouraged me to write about my feelings. They both went back to Dr. Murray with me for three months to continue working on their understanding of my issues and why the effects of bullying still remained nine months after it happened. Dr. Murray also helped me to remember that I had to take personal responsibility for my reactions. I learned to ask for assistance and understanding. I also learned how much to tell people and to whom I could safely talk when I needed help.

When I finally started talking about everything, I realized that Morgan's bullying actually started in kindergarten. She had told other people that I was crazy. I hadn't told Mom or anyone else about it at the time. Now I knew that I had tolerated Morgan's abuse because I so desperately wanted my peers at Manuoku to accept me. While I always had Lei, I did have trouble making new friends. Nicole was my only true friend at Manuoku prior to sixth grade.

In sixth grade, Lei and Nicole helped me to make new friends. As my confidence grew and I realized who the good kids were, I found out all of the kids in my school orchestra were nice people.

I continued to play the cello in the orchestra and to take piano lessons with Mr. Wang. I was also studying music composition and was composing simple songs, but my goal was still to write a symphony.

Life was going much better. When I thought about everything, I wished I had known sooner about what to tell and what not to tell people. I hoped that one day, others would support and understand sensory issues the same way they supported and understood people who had a physical illness or injury.

Part of me wanted to become an advocate for all of the kids who were delightfully different like me. *Delightfully different* was what Mom called me. I still wasn't brave enough to speak up. I didn't trust people enough yet. I wanted to believe there were good people who would understand; unfortunately, our society seemed mean to me. There were TV shows where people ambushed their "friends," so they could tell them how awfully they dressed. There were people who posted things on the Internet about my generation. They said, "This generation needs to get tougher. Their parents overprotect them. There has always been bullying of kids who are different."

They said that those of us who were different just needed to learn to fit in, as if it were our fault that we were mistreated. They didn't think that society should make accommodations for us at all. They implied that our sensory issues were something that our overprotective parents invented. They even blamed our parents for our sensory issues.

Our society was advancing technically, but it was returning to an age of barbarians in terms of the way we treated others. Honestly, what gave anyone the right to judge what I or anyone else wore? Why should I have to be just like everyone else? More important, why would I want to?

Francesca

I agreed with Mia. Our society would bully the greatest minds in history if they lived today. Perhaps they would have lost their confidence as a result. Maybe we wouldn't have the works of William Shakespeare if he lived now. Maybe Van Gogh would have destroyed his artwork before he killed himself. Maybe Alexander Graham Bell would have never invented the telephone, and we wouldn't have cell phones and text messages. Mozart could have burned all of his music and gone on a killing spree instead of writing his great symphonies. Benjamin Franklin might have kept flying his kite. Lightning might have struck him dead. Would we all still use candles now? Who knows?

I really didn't want to know how our world would have looked without the delightfully different people throughout history. What I knew was what my parents taught me: to treat others as I wanted to be treated, as the Bible said. They also taught me to be tolerant of others' differences and at the very least to never be mean. Somehow, a large portion of our society had forgotten the golden rule. Instead, they thought being mean should be the norm, especially if the person they were mean to was someone who looked or acted differently than they did.

Frankly, I found this behavior scary. This was how Hitler acted when he slaughtered the Jews too. This type of thinking has always caused people to be meaner and meaner.

In Rwanda, it resulted in mass murder when the Hutu massacred the Tutsi. The Hutu felt that the Tutsi were unfairly elevated to a ruling class by the Belgian colonists, and when the Hutu later came into power, the rift between the two grew until the anger lead to genocide. It was all about perceived differences.

This was the excuse school shooters used for killing others too. I decided we needed to change this. It was time we learned from our mistakes. We needed to learn tolerance and forgiveness instead of meanness and revenge.

I sincerely hoped enough people would see how wrong being mean to others was before our society got worse. I liked to think there were still good people in our society. I sincerely hoped enough people would speak up against meanness to make a positive change before our society escalated into worse violence. I prayed we learned lessons from the distant past as well as from more recent events in Rwanda, Bosnia, Iraq, and Israel and in other parts of the world.

People have always said that we have freedom in this country. They believed in freedom of speech. Yet even in America, we still had people who were so prejudiced that they were mean. We had people who wanted to blame others for their problems. They wanted everyone to be just like them.

Mia's grandpa taught me that there were good and bad people everywhere. I knew this was true. I hoped and prayed that there were more good than bad. I hoped one day people would accept others for who they were, not who they wanted them to be. I hoped Mia's generation would one day learn to heal all prejudice.

In the meantime, we had to make changes where we could and forgive ignorance as much as possible. Otherwise, we risked becoming the mean ones.

*   *   *

"Mom I knew you were right. Believe me, I was trying to forgive. I knew I never wanted to wound anyone the way people had wounded me. Morgan still had friends. I didn't believe my avoiding her was harming her in any way. I wasn't avoiding her to hurt her. I was avoiding her to protect myself. I just wished other people understood this. I couldn't really explain it to them without sounding mean."

"Mia, I think you just needed more time to heal. Plus, you really didn't have to be friends with Morgan to forgive her."

"Yes, I knew that, and I was getting there. I was also trying hard to forgive Dad for your sake. I knew he still loved me. I didn't hate him anymore. It was just that I still had a hard time trusting him, as he never seemed to understand me. I could see that he was trying. Mom, so was I."

"The best gift I could ever receive would be to have you and your father close again. I hoped that one day you would forgive him for not understanding. After all, you forgave me."

"I already promised to try."

"That was a start. He also promised to be more patient with you. I hoped one day you would both remember how much you loved each other."

Epilogue

I had made it! I was a senior. I had maintained a 4.0 average at Manuoku. New York was waiting for me. Julliard had given me a full music scholarship in composition. I worked with my cello teacher and another composer, and I copyrighted my first symphony. Our school orchestra would be performing it during our graduation ceremony. It was truly amazing!

Dad was my biggest fan now since I kept my promise to Mom to work on our relationship. I finally forgave him at the end of seventh grade. I had talked to him about everything since then. As always, Mom knew best.

I even managed to forgive Morgan. However, since we didn't have anything in common, we weren't friends. Forgiving her helped me to overcome my anger about the past so I could move on with my life.

I forgave Ah Ma and Ah Gung too. They were so proud of me for my accomplishments, but now I knew that they would have loved me no matter what I did. Thanks, Mom. You were right again.

I also learned that spending time with real friends was fun. Yes, during the last six years of school, I made amazing friends. My best friends were still Lei and Nicole. They were there through the best and worst of times. They even encouraged me to pursue my music.

Lei too got a full scholarship to Julliard, although her scholarship was in dance, not music. We were to be roommates. Nicole was going to New York too, although she was going to Columbia as a pre-law major. We would all still get to see each other. Who could have ever asked for more?

Except there was more—I had a boyfriend who would be going to Julliard too. Of course, Mom and Dad made me promise my studies would still come first. My boyfriend even understood this. The next chapter of my life was where he would be.

*　　*　　*

"You made us so proud! I loved that you were so close to your dad again. I always knew your future would be bright. I just wished you weren't going to be so far away. Of course, I would be sure to visit and to send tickets for you to return home during your breaks. I was so glad that Lei would be with you at Julliard and that Nicole would be close by. Who knew that Manuoku had such talented kids?

"Of course, I always knew that at least one of Manuoku's kids was amazing. I think once the school started valuing differences, it allowed all of you to shine."

*　　*　　*

Francesca

Now it was time to turn my focus to Cal. He became the other amazing child in the Lung family. He starred in a high school musical at Skylark last year and he too hoped to one day go to Julliard. Go figure! Ben and I had produced two very talented, amazing, delightful children.

Cal gets to be the star in the next novel, but Mia will have a part too—after all, I have to tell you how she met her boyfriend.

To all of you delightfully different kids, continue supporting each other so you too can achieve your dreams. Anything is possible if you believe in yourself and if you are surrounded by the love of family and friends.

To all of you mainstreamers, do not despair; there is hope for you also as long as you remember to treat others the way you want to be treated. Remember, that oddball kid may one day be a star. Maybe you will get to work for him or her.

Resources

Attwood, Tony. 2007. *The Complete Guide to Asperger's Syndrome*. London: Jessica Kingsley Publishers.

Attwood, Tony, and Temple Grandin. 2006. *Asperger's and Girls*. Arlington, Texas: Future Horizons.

Holliday Willey, Liane. 1999. *Pretending to Be Normal: Living with Asperger's Syndrome*. London: Jessica Kingsley Publishers.

Romanowski Bashe, Patricia, and Barbara L. Kirby. 2005. *The OASIS Guide to Asperger Syndrome*. New York: Crown Publishers.

Sicile-Kira, Chantal. 2006. *Adolescents on the Autism Spectrum: A Parent's Guide to the Cognitive, Social, Physical, and Transition Needs of Teenagers with Autism Spectrum Disorders*. New York, New York: Penguin Group.

Silverman, Stephan M., and Rich Weinfeld. 2007. *School Success for Kids with Asperger's Syndrome*. Waco, Texas: Prufrock Press Inc.

Smith Myles, Brenda, Katherine Tapscott Cook, Nancy E. Miller, Louann Rinner, and Lisa A. Robbins. 2000. *Asperger Syndrome and Sensory Issues: Practical Solutions for Making Sense of the World*. Shawnee Mission, Kansas: Autism Asperger Publishing Co.

Yoshida, Yuko. 2007. *How to Be Yourself in a World That's Different*. London: Jessica Kingsley Publishers.

D. S. WALKER has been a registered nurse for over twenty-five years and has extensively studied sensory processing issues related to Asperger's Syndrome. She lives in Honolulu, Hawaii, with her husband and two children, where she enjoys spending time with family and friends, walking her dogs, and reading.

CPSIA information can be obtained at www.ICGtesting.com
Printed in the USA
BVOW05s2158171115

427056BV00004B/168/P